THE KEYS OF LOVE

As soon as Romany was well out of earshot, Lady Butterclere leaned menacingly towards Henrietta.

"Now you just take heed, Miss Reed. I know your sort only too well. You intercepted that note. You aim to set your cap at the Duke and distract him from Romany."

"I c-can assure you, such a thought was n-never on my mind."

"Was it not?" asked Lady Butterclere sarcastically. "Then would you explain to me why you were on your way to see the Duke *in that provocative condition?*"

For a moment, she was horribly confused. What did Lady Butterclere mean *in that provocative condition?*

With dawning horror, she remembered that she had not been able to hook up her dress – she had rushed out of Kitty's room without asking for help.

Now she glanced into the mirror on the stairs and almost burst into tears at the sight that met her eyes.

Her hair had come loose and now fell over her face untidily. Her dress had slipped off, exposing an alabaster shoulder and the tip of a heaving breast.

What was more, she had forgotten to put on any stockings or shoes and was standing there in her bare feet.

"Oh. Oh. Oh," she cried.

"I should think so too," said Lady Butterclere with grim satisfaction. "You look like a – *a common harlot!*"

THE BARBARA CARTLAND PINK COLLECTION

Titles in this series

THE KEYS OF LOVE

BARBARA CARTLAND

Barbaracartland.com Ltd

THE BARBARA CARTLAND PINK COLLECTION

Barbara Cartland was the most prolific bestselling author in the history of the world. She was frequently in the Guinness Book of Records for writing more books in a year than any other living author. In fact her most amazing literary feat was when her publishers asked for more Barbara Cartland romances, she doubled her output from 10 books a year to over 20 books a year, when she was 77.

She went on writing continuously at this rate for 20 years and wrote her last book at the age of 97, thus completing 400 books between the ages of 77 and 97.

Her publishers finally could not keep up with this phenomenal output, so at her death she left 160 unpublished manuscripts, something again that no other author has ever achieved.

Now the exciting news is that these 160 original unpublished Barbara Cartland books are already being published and by Barbaracartland.com exclusively on the internet, as the international web is the best possible way of reaching so many Barbara Cartland readers around the world.

The 160 books are published monthly and will be numbered in sequence.

The series is called the Pink Collection as a tribute to Barbara Cartland whose favourite colour was pink and it became very much her trademark over the years.

The Barbara Cartland Pink Collection is published only on the internet. Log on to www.barbaracartland.com to find out how you can purchase the books monthly as they are published, and take out a subscription that will ensure that all subsequent editions are delivered to you by mail order to your home.

NEW

Barbaracartland.com is proud to announce the publication of ten new Audio Books for the first time as CDs. They are favourite Barbara Cartland stories read by well-known actors and actresses and each story extends to 4 or 5 CDs. The Audio Books are as follows:

The Patient Bridegroom	The Passion and the Flower
A Challenge of Hearts	Little White Doves of Love
A Train to Love	The Prince and the Pekinese
The Unbroken Dream	A King in Love
The Cruel Count	A Sign of Love

More Audio Books will be published in the future and the above titles can be purchased by logging on to the website www.barbaracartland.com or please write to the address below.

If you do not have access to a computer, you can write for information about the Barbara Cartland Pink Collection and the Barbara Cartland Audio Books to the following address:

Barbara Cartland.com Ltd., Camfield Place,
Hatfield, Hertfordshire AL9 6JE, United Kingdom.
Telephone: +44 (0)1707 642629
Fax: +44 (0)1707 663041

THE LATE DAME BARBARA CARTLAND

Barbara Cartland who sadly died in May 2000 at the age of nearly 99 was the world's most famous romantic novelist who wrote 723 books in her lifetime with worldwide sales of over 1 billion copies and her books were translated into 36 different languages.

As well as romantic novels, she wrote historical biographies, 6 autobiographies, theatrical plays, books of advice on life, love, vitamins and cookery. She also found time to be a political speaker and television and radio personality.

She wrote her first book at the age of 21 and this was called *Jigsaw*. It became an immediate bestseller and sold 100,000 copies in hardback and was translated into 6 different languages. She wrote continuously throughout her life, writing bestsellers for an astonishing 76 years. Her books have always been immensely popular in the United States, where in 1976 her current books were at numbers 1 & 2 in the B. Dalton bestsellers list, a feat never achieved before or since by any author.

Barbara Cartland became a legend in her own lifetime and will be best remembered for her wonderful romantic novels, so loved by her millions of readers throughout the world.

Her books will always be treasured for their moral message, her pure and innocent heroines, her good looking and dashing heroes and above all her belief that the power of love is more important than anything else in everyone's life.

"We all seek love, but never never try too hard to find the keys of love, because love will find you in the end and often in the most unexpected way.

Barbara Cartland

CHAPTER ONE
1890

Henrietta Radford stifled the urge to yawn.

Straight above the head of Count Majstorovic, who was kneeling passionately in front of her, she could see her reflection in the mirror across the room.

An eighteen-year old girl with long blonde tresses and sea-green eyes in a grey dress and pretty red boots.

She gave a start as the Count suddenly grasped her hand and dragged it to his fervid lips.

His minute kisses made her think of mosquito bites and she disengaged her hand with a barely disguised flinch.

The Count looked at her questioningly.

"You do not – like me?"

Henrietta swallowed.

There was nothing at all particularly wrong with the Count, but there was nothing particularly right either. His jowls quivered when he became heated and his hands were large and ungainly and the colour of smoked ham.

And she did think that large sword he insisted on wearing as part of his Bulgarian Army costume was rather preposterous.

He looked so like a figure from feudal Europe when this was Boston, United States of America, 1890!

"Miss Radford, my cherub, won't you answer me?"

Henrietta sighed.

"I'm so sorry, Count, but you see – you are suitor number four this week and I get rather muddled!"

The Count bridled.

"There are others?"

"Oh, yes," replied Henrietta mournfully. *"Many."*

The Count rose majestically.

"Then I salute you and withdraw. When a young lady does not see the virtue of a Bulgarian, she is blind!"

The Count bowed, clicked his heels and was gone.

Henrietta had been living in America for two and a half years, but it was only in the last months that she had been able to purchase some superb items for her wardrobe.

She gave another sigh and leaned back in her chair.

Despite the pleasure of such luxuries as handmade boots, she had grown tired of life in Boston.

She missed England and her home there, Lushwood Manor, even though she and father had left it under very sad circumstances.

Lushwood had once been a beacon for elegance and gaiety. Many lavish balls were held there when old Lord Radford – Henrietta's grandfather – was alive.

She recalled creeping out of the nursery in order to gaze down through the banisters of the great stairway at the guests arriving. Lords and Ladies, Dukes and Duchesses, Counts and Countesses.

She remembered one night in particular.

Her mother was playing French airs on the piano in the drawing room and the sound drifted into the hall where a young man had just arrived late and was in the process of removing his cape.

He was very tall with raven black hair and a strong profile. He looked every inch a Prince out of a storybook.

Catching sight of the little girl peering breathlessly down at him, the young man gave a conspiratorial wink.

"What, are you not dancing this evening?" he asked mischievously.

Henrietta shook her head.

"I am not allowed into the parlour at this hour," she explained shyly.

The young man thought for a moment.

"But you are allowed into the hall at this hour?"

Henrietta considered gravely.

"I think so. Nobody has ever said I shouldn't!"

The young man held out his hand.

"Then why not come down and waltz with me?"

The housemaid in the hall looked disapproving, but Henrietta did not care.

She tripped lightly down the stairs, holding up her night shift as if it was the most beautiful ball gown.

"It isn't quite a waltz that is being played," said the young man. "We will have to improvise!"

Henrietta did not know what the word 'improvise' meant, but she said nothing.

She just placed her hand in her partner's and they were away.

The housemaid watched with pursed lips, throwing anxious glances at her, but she did not notice.

She felt like a feather, drifting here and there over the floor.

So this was what it was like to be grown-up!

When the dance finished, the young man bowed.

"Thank you, Miss Radford. I presume you are Miss Radford and not some changeling?"

Henrietta, unsure of 'changeling', but being certain of who she was, nodded proudly.

"And how old are you, Miss Radford?"

"Seven," replied Henrietta gravely. "And a half."

Her partner's eyes twinkled.

"Well, when you are seven*teen* and a half, we will hopefully dance again."

Henrietta had often thought since of the handsome young man who had danced so gracefully with her, but she never saw him again.

Perhaps it was because those days of splendour at Lushwood had ended soon after, when her grandfather died and it was discovered that he had squandered a large part of the family fortunes.

For years the new young Lord Radford and his wife struggled to maintain the house and its extensive estate.

Then Lady Radford died and Lord Radford lost all heart for the task. Day after day, Henrietta would find her father in his study, a glass of wine in his hand, as he stared disconsolately at the lovely portrait of his late wife.

Henrietta blinked away her own tears whenever she looked at the portrait.

Her mother had been regarded as something of a Saint. She had weathered the vicissitudes of her husband's wealth with equanimity. She neither admonished him for his generosity to impoverished relations, nor pilloried him when that generosity was not returned in his hour of need.

Henrietta had always believed her mother to be the prettiest woman in the world with her thick dark hair and warm hazel eyes.

One morning, looking up at her portrait, Henrietta thought she could see something else in those eyes. There seemed to be an expression of deep concern in them as she gazed down upon her grieving husband.

She followed her mother's gaze to where her father slumped in his chair, his glass of wine at such an angle that it seemed it must spill on the carpet.

Gently Henrietta reached out and took the glass out of her father's hand.

"Papa. Please don't be so sad. Mama would not be happy to see you like this."

Lord Radford repressed a sob as he replied,

"Ah, my dear, how can I not be sad? I have lost the dearest sweetest companion. She was always delicate, but to be stolen from me by a fever – just a fever! How can I ever recover? No marriage was ever so content as mine. Now I have no one. *No one!*"

"You have *me*, Papa," whispered Henrietta.

Lord Radford put his hand over his face in remorse.

"Child, how can I be so insensitive! Of course, I have you, but one day you will marry and leave me."

"Everybody leaves in the end, Papa, so that there is always somebody who is left behind."

He twisted in his chair to regard his daughter with astonishment.

"Those are sad but wise words for one so young!"

Henrietta was fifteen and a half, but, as she looked back at her father now, she felt much older.

"Papa," she said, "let's go out and prune the roses in Mama's garden. They look so terribly overgrown."

Her father roused himself to do as she suggested, realising that he had somewhat neglected her in his all-consuming grief.

He could not lose his air of dejection, however, and Henrietta despaired as summer waned and the trees began to shed their leaves.

A long sad winter lay ahead.

*

Then one autumn morning a letter arrived bearing a very unfamiliar postmark.

"*The – United States – of America*," Henrietta read out with surprise before handing the letter to her father.

"My goodness," he exclaimed, "it must be from my old uncle Harold. He emigrated some thirty years ago and has not been heard of since."

The letter was not from Uncle Harold, but from his lawyer.

Uncle Harold had died, bequeathing his nephew a large tract of land in Texas.

To Lord Radford, this seemed like a sign, a chance to leave the sadness of Lushwood behind for a while.

He decided he must travel to Texas and attempt to establish a farm there.

"Many people make fortunes in America!" he cried. "Think of how Lushwood would benefit if I was to return with loads of money!"

Henrietta begged to go with him and not to be left behind in a boarding school.

Too fond of his daughter to thwart her, he agreed.

Lushwood was closed and most of what remained of the staff, a cook and two scullery maids, were dismissed.

Henrietta's old nanny, however, was recalled from retirement to travel to America with them.

Nanny readily assented, for she had been missing young Henrietta a great deal.

Lord Radford, Henrietta and Nanny left Lushwood on a grey autumnal morning.

Henrietta leaned out of the carriage window for a

last glimpse of her beloved home, which bore a dilapidated and abandoned air.

'We'll be back,' she whispered. 'I promise we'll be back. And then you'll be restored to all your former glory – just as Mama would have wished!'

At first it had not seemed that her promise would ever be fulfilled.

The land in Texas turned out to be dry and thorny. All efforts to farm the land successfully had failed.

Lord Radford and the local Mexicans he employed toiled day and night, but neither crop nor cattle flourished.

Henrietta and Nanny did their best to keep order in the house, a big rambling adobe, ranch-style building, but the heat and flies seemed to affect everyone.

Henrietta's one consolation was that her father had to work so hard on the farm that his mind could not dwell very often on the loss of his adored wife.

Then, one evening, one of the Mexican farmhands, Pablo, came running to the house in great excitement. He must speak to the 'Meester'.

Lord Radford had left Pablo sinking a new well to the North of the farm.

"I dig deeper and deeper and stop to wipe my face," babbled Pablo, "and when I take up my spade again, what is coming out of the earth at my feet – but plenty water!

"Plenty. Only it ees thick. And *black*. Black as my kettle. It bubbles up, Meester, as if eet has no end!"

Lord Radford had leaped up in an instant. He knew what that meant.

Oil!

He was now a wealthy man!

The fortunes of the Radfords had turned at last.

Too late, alas, to save his wife! But not too late to save Lushwood and to ensure a comfortable future for his darling daughter.

Henrietta was sent North to Boston, where she was lodged with Nanny and attended a finishing school. She was sorry to leave her father, but not dusty Texas.

She made good friends among her schoolmates, but after six months she felt 'finished' enough.

She had learned posture and etiquette and how to sit with her hands in her lap, but her mind hungered for more substantial fare.

Left to her own devices in the big house on Boston Common, she read all she could lay her hands on, and even taught herself to speak French.

Her father visited when he could, but she knew that he was busy sinking wells and building up his business and she would have dearly loved to see more of him.

Meanwhile, as news of the oil find on the Radford land spread North, Henrietta found herself besieged by a growing number of suitors.

Most were from impoverished European Royalty or aristocracy come to America to marry into money.

There just seemed to be a virtual epidemic of these men offering some title or other in return for a fat dowry.

One day she was beginning to dream wistfully of a man who would love her for something other than the large number of gold nuggets stacking up in her father's account in the Bank of North America.

She started from her reveries when the door of the drawing room opened and Nanny put her head round.

"It's a lovely bright day, my dear. Would you care to go skating?"

Henrietta jumped up in delight.

"Oh yes, Poody!"

Poody was her chidhood pet name for Nanny.

It had been snowing all morning, but now the sun was out and the frozen pond was shining like pewter.

She sailed gaily onto the ice, her hands enveloped in a thick white muff. Soon her cheeks were rosy red and her eyes sparkling.

Blonde curls fluttered about her face though most of her hair was tucked into a soft white fur hat.

Nanny thought that she looked a delightful picture in the pale winter sunlight.

There was a delicate crunch of snow underfoot as a gentleman wearing a cloak and a black racoon hat came to the edge of the pond. He lit up a big cigar and stood there, smoking and watching Henrietta.

She was not aware of him at first as her eyes were half closed as she whirled and twirled, feeling wonderfully alone in this powdery sparkling kingdom.

It was only when she skated closer to the shore that her gaze fell on her watcher.

His intense stare unnerved her and before she knew it she was wobbling dangerously.

Next she landed unceremoniously on her back.

Henrietta heard Nanny's gasp and then she could hear someone else slide out onto the ice.

A second later the gentleman in the racoon hat was hovering over her, his cigar still smoking in his hand.

"You are not hurt?" he enquired.

"N-no. I don't think, I am," murmured Henrietta.

"Well, please, allow me to help you to your feet."

He threw aside the cigar and extended his hand.

Henrietta was lifted up and guided onto the bank.

Nanny fussed around her, removing her skates and shaking the powdery ice from her muff.

Henrietta stood still mutely, glancing up from under her long lashes at the handsome stranger.

For he was indeed handsome in a very sharp way.

His lips and nose were delineated like cut glass and his eyebrows were quite straight. His eyes were blue and might have seemed frosty to other observers, but Henrietta was only aware of the searching interest they betrayed.

'Well,' she thought, 'at least he likes me – and I think he *does* like me – for myself alone, for he has no idea of who I am.'

"Your home is far?" he asked with evident concern. It was clear from his accent that he was not American.

"No, very close," replied Henrietta. "We are just over there. The house with yellow shutters."

The gentleman followed her eye.

Henrietta gave him no chance to enquire her name. She did not wish to spoil the pleasure of being admired for herself alone.

Back in her little red boots and galoshes and her muff restored, she quickly bid the stranger adieu.

When she glanced over her shoulder as she left the common with Nanny, he was still watching her.

*

The very next morning she heard the doorbell ring.

A moment later a maid came into the drawing room to announce that Prince Vasily of Rumania requested the pleasure of calling upon the young lady with the red boots and the white fur hat.

It was clearly the gentleman from the day before.

'*And he still does not have any idea of who I am,*' thought Henrietta in delight.

10

Prince Vasily was dressed in scarlet and clicked his heels when he greeted her.

"You now know my name," he began, "but I am at the disadvantage, for I do not know yours."

Henrietta hesitated.

"It is Henrietta Radford," she replied at last, staring up at him.

She waited for an instant gleam of recognition, for the inevitable glitter of pecuniary interest to enter his eyes as with so many of her suitors, but it did not come.

"Radford?" he repeated. "I think you are not native to Boston, no?"

"No," she breathed. "I am English. My father is in Texas for a while – on business."

"I wish him success, for Texas is hard country."

Convinced that here at last was a man who had no interest in her fortune, the next hour passed like a dream.

She learned that the Prince was travelling the world before he settled down to administer his estate near Okna, in the foothills of the Carpathian Mountains.

When the Prince begged leave to call on her again, Henrietta was happy to accede to his wish.

Even Nanny approved.

The Prince took to calling every morning and soon he and Henrietta were driving out together in his splendidly upholstered carriage.

One morning he sighed as he looked out upon the snowy streets of Boston.

"In my country now, there is also much snow, and the mountains are looking like pillars of ice."

"It sounds as if it's very beautiful there," murmured Henrietta.

"It is beautiful, but – " the Prince heaved a deeper sigh, "mine is a Kingdom that is lacking a Princess!"

With a thrill Henrietta realised that the Prince was now seriously courting her.

Since he had not known her name when they first met and therefore could not possibly be a fortune hunter, Henrietta allowed herself to take his attentions seriously.

She began to imagine herself as a Princess, strolling the grounds of Okna on the arm of her handsome husband.

She found herself blushing whenever he raised her hand to his lips or fixed an especially ardent gaze on her.

She was very excited when her father wired to say he would be arriving that weekend for a short visit.

She could not wait to introduce him to the Prince.

He was almost the first subject raised as her father set down his case in the hall on his arrival.

"He is very aristocratic, Papa, and his manners are impeccable! And he must have a fortune of his own, for he rides in a fancy carriage. He is just as a Prince should be!"

"Is he, indeed!" smiled her father, handing his hat to the maid.

He was only too well aware of the many greedy and unscrupulous men who had been endlessly plying her with their attentions for the last twelve months.

"Oh, he is, Papa. And the best thing is – he had no idea who I was when I first met him and no idea who I was when he first called on me."

Here the maid gave a little start and almost dropped the hat.

However, neither her father nor Henrietta noticed.

"So you see, Papa," she went on, "he must like me for myself alone, mustn't he?"

"I suppose so – " he replied, removing his coat.

Lord Radford followed her into the drawing room.

"And how is Nanny?" he asked.

"Oh, she is somewhat under the weather these last two days. She has remained in bed."

Not wishing him to worry, she plunged on quickly.

"She says she's feeling better already, although she won't come down to greet you until tomorrow morning."

Palms under his chin, he now regarded his daughter fondly. She was wearing a pretty dress of pink and white gingham and a white ribbon held back her blonde locks.

"I do declare, Henrietta, you are turning into quite the American girl!" he teased.

"Papa, I'm not – am I?"

Lord Radford laughed.

"Well, perhaps not quite – yet. If we are here for much longer, though – "

"Papa, don't torment me. I like American girls and I like America. It's just – that I don't want to feel like a stranger when we go home. I will be going home one day, won't I, Papa?"

"Well, I have some news in that respect that I think will please you."

"What is it, Papa?"

"I have been training a manager to take over from me in the business. You and I will be able to return home before the end of the year and start renovating Lushwood!"

"Oh, Papa, will we really?" breathed Henrietta in great excitement.

"Yes. I have been compiling a list of architects to help us. We cannot book our passage just yet, but we *can* start thinking about the improvements we would like."

"That is wonderful news. However – "

Henrietta's face suddenly fell.

"I wonder if England will be on Prince Vasily's itinerary?"

'Ah!' mused Lord Radford, regarding his daughter closely. 'So that's the way of it! I had better meet this fellow without any delay, it seems!'

"Shall we then invite him to supper and find out?"

Henrietta clapped her hands in delight.

Later that evening, she and her father were waiting in the drawing room for the Prince to arrive when the maid knocked and entered.

With a glance at Henrietta, she asked if she might speak privately with Lord Radford.

He rose and followed her out into the corridor.

Henrietta looked up at her father when he returned after several minutes.

"What is it, Papa?" she asked, as he stood regarding her with evident concern.

"There is something you should know," he began, and then the doorbell rang loudly.

Henrietta sprang up.

"There he is, Papa. Now you will see! But what is it that I must know – ?"

"It must wait until later," he murmured, listening to the sound of the maid hurrying to the front door.

As the Prince strode in, Henrietta thought he looked so distinguished with his scarlet jacket and white gloves.

She was perturbed at the slight frown that hovered on her father's brow, but it was gone in an instant.

All evening he was the perfect host and all evening Prince Vasily was the perfect guest, appreciative, attentive, and full of polite conversation.

When Henrietta asked him eagerly if England was on his itinerary, he remarked elegantly that it surely would be if she was there.

When at last the Prince left after a glass of brandy and a cigar with Lord Radford, Henrietta could not wait to discover her father's impression.

She burst into the library.

"Papa!"

Lord Radford looked up.

"My dear?"

"*Papa*! Tell me, please. What did you think of my Prince?"

Her father regarded her gravely.

"It's what *you* think of him that troubles me."

Henrietta frowned.

"*Troubles* you? Why?"

Her father sighed and reached for the decanter.

"You like him a great deal, I know, but how do you know he is all that he says he is?"

"How do I know? Why because – because – it's he who tells me so."

Lord Radford shook his head.

"But my dear, I'm afraid that I have to tell you that he is an accomplished dissembler."

He might as well have struck his daughter.

She paled and stepped back.

"Di – ssembler? How do you know?"

In answer, he rose, went to the door and called for the maid.

Henrietta stared at him feeling bewildered. He did not speak until the maid appeared, her eyes cast down.

"Will you now repeat to my daughter what you told me earlier," he urged wearily.

The maid clasped and unclasped her hands.

"It was when I heard Miss Henrietta say the Prince didn't know who she was when he first called at the house, I thought, hadn't I better speak up? You see I had noticed him weeks ago, driving by the house time after time in that carriage.

"Then I heard he was asking questions around the district. He knew who she was all right and only yesterday I heard from the baker, who heard it from the farrier, that the carriage and the get-up are all hired. It's said round the town that he has hardly a cent to his name. He's a fortune seeker, sure as apples are green!"

There was a long silence, whilst the maid twisted her hands together, worrying as to whether she had done the right thing or not.

Henrietta stood for a long time feeling tearful.

"Oh, dear," she spoke at last in a low sad voice. "I-I've been rather a fool, haven't I!"

"I sure am sorry, miss," said the maid.

"That's alright," Henrietta told her soberly. "You were – right to tell me. When the Prince calls tomorrow, do not on any account let him in. And now – I must go to bed. Goodnight, Papa."

Her father hesitated before he answered.

"Goodnight, my dearest," he said gently, impressed with his daughter's composure.

He was not to hear her sobbing later in her room, as she pressed her face into her pillow to stifle the sound.

*

The next day, Lord Radford went to visit the bank.

Henrietta did not go with him, as she felt somewhat fatigued. She had not slept at all well.

She was sewing quietly in the drawing room when the doorbell sounded and she held her breath, listening.

Yes, it was Prince Vasily.

She recognised his exclamation of surprise as the maid informed him that her Mistress was not at home.

Then there was the sound of the door being closed.

She breathed out in relief and took up her sewing.

Only a few minutes had passed when she heard the squeak of the gate in the yard at the back of the house.

She sat, hand poised over her sampler.

Was that someone mounting the iron stairway that led to the first floor balcony?

Was that a shadow by the drawing room window?

Was somebody there?

She was about to put down her sampler and reach for the bell when the window was thrown open and a pair of highly polished boots appeared over the low sill.

Prince Vasily followed!

"H-how dare you!" she gasped, rising in horror.

She reached again for the bell pull, but the Prince sprang forward and threw himself at her feet.

"Please, you must hear me," he moaned. "My heart is burning. Why do you not wish to see me today, why?"

"It's not just for *today* I do not wish to see you," asserted Henrietta, trying hard to suppress the tremor in her voice. "It's forever."

"*Forever?*"

The Prince stared in disbelief.

"What means this?"

She noticed for the first time, as she gazed down at him, that the end of his nose was as thin as a knife blade.

"It means," she answered as calmly as she could, "that I am – no longer deceived."

"Deceived!"

The Prince rose magisterially from his knees.

"How do I deceive you? I am impassioned for you. *Impassioned*!"

He did indeed appear impassioned, his nostrils were quivering and his pupils burning with ardour.

"I'm so sorry if you are, Prince, for I am not!"

"You refuse me? It is quite impossible," he cried and with that he lunged forward to embrace her.

Her sampler and its sharp pin was an impediment.

"Oooch!" yelped the Prince, holding up a palm on which a bead of blood had instantly appeared.

"I am afraid I can only think it serves you right," said Henrietta, in what she hoped was an icy tone. "Now you must please leave or I shall call one of the servants."

It was at this very moment that the Prince appeared to metamorphose before her very eyes.

All ardour – so obviously feigned – was gone in a flash.

His lips tightened until they seemed a thread drawn under his moustache. His eyes hardened like hailstones.

"You would call a servant to remove *me*?"

"Y-yes. C-certainly," replied Henrietta, unnerved by the malice now apparent in the Prince's demeanour.

"Nobody threatens this to Prince Vasily," he hissed. "*Nobody*. I will go, but you will regret such treatment of me. This I promise!"

Henrietta trembled as he put his face close to hers.

"I will make sure you suffer for this," he grunted through gritted teeth.

Then he turned and was gone the way he had come.

Henrietta felt faint.

She had never in her life encountered such hostility, nor endured such a threatening volte-face of behaviour.

She was afraid he had cursed her and she wished to get as far away from him and his kind as possible.

She had had enough of this long line of importunate deceivers.

When she heard the sound of her father's voice in the hall, she groped her way thankfully to the door of the drawing room.

"Papa!"

Lord Radford turned and started at the sight of his daughter, wide-eyed and trembling.

"Henrietta! What on earth is the matter, my dear?"

She took several unsteady steps towards her father before collapsing with a sob into his arms.

"I want to go home, Papa. Not in a few months or a few weeks, but *tomorrow*. Please, Papa, please. I mean it with all my heart. *I want to go home*!"

CHAPTER TWO

Henrietta and her father stood at the railings on the first class deck of *The Boston Queen.*

Nanny was below, ensuring their trunks containing Henrietta's wardrobe were delivered to the right cabin.

Lord Radford had booked her passage on a ship that sailed only two days after the incident with Prince Vasily.

Henrietta felt no sadness as she gazed at the Boston skyline. It was not her home and she had few friends.

"Well, the cabins are fancy enough," came Nanny's voice. "No better than they should be for a Radford!"

Henrietta's father turned with a quick frown.

"You are forgetting yourself, Nanny. Remember, that for the purposes of this voyage, she is not Henrietta Radford. She is Miss *Harrietta Reed.*"

Nanny looked crestfallen.

"Oh, dearie me, my poor old head."

He had decided that it would be best for Henrietta to travel incognito on the ship in order to avoid the kind of attentions that were driving her out of Boston.

He also wished to spare her the embarrassment of being met at Liverpool by various gentlemen of the press.

The story of the English Lord who had struck oil in America had already been reported in *The Times* and any reporter worth his salt would consider it quite a scoop to interview Henrietta on her arrival home.

Lord Radford could not leave his business as yet, as he was still training up a manager to take his place.

He would follow Henrietta as soon as he could.

"I hope *you* remember that your name is now Miss Reed," he was saying to Henrietta. "That is the name you are booked under, after all."

"I'll remember," she answered. "And I'll certainly remember that Nanny is now *Mrs.Poody*!"

It was decided as well that Nanny should travel as a companion to Miss Reed to further protect her identity.

Nanny gave a cross little shake of her shoulders at being Mrs. Poody. She would have liked something a little more dignified than a childish nickname.

However, she could not be annoyed for more than a second with her beloved charge.

Lord Radford took out his watch.

"Almost time," he intoned with a sad glance at his daughter.

The long queue of passengers tripping up the three gangways for First Class, Second Class and Steerage had by now slowed down to a trickle.

It was therefore easy to see the sudden last minute flurry of figures that spilled out of the departure building and hurried towards the ship.

Henrietta watched as they scrambled up the Second Class gangway. They were in black overcoats and carried leather containers of various shapes and sizes.

"It must be the ship's orchestra," commented Lord Radford, following his daughter's gaze. "And those are their instruments."

"An orchestra!" murmured Henrietta. "What fun!"

One member of the orchestra had lingered behind on the quayside. He seemed to be waiting for someone, as he

21

had his back to the ship and was eagerly scanning the departure building.

The ship's horn blew – a long and mournful sound.

"I must disembark," said Lord Radford softly.

Henrietta threw herself into her father's arms.

"Goodbye, dearest Papa, I shall miss you so. But you will follow soon, won't you?"

"As soon as I can, my darling," he promised.

He winked at Nanny.

"You'll keep a close eye on my treasure, won't you, Mrs. Poody?"

Nanny suppressed a giggle.

"Oh, don't worry, I won't let her out of my sight!"

Henrietta and Nanny waved as he walked down the gangway. He turned on the quay and stood there, waiting.

The ship's horn blew again.

The lone member of the orchestra on the quayside looked again at his watch as a sailor called down to him that they were about to raise the gangway.

Shaking his head, he pocketed his watch and began to climb, not the Second Class gangway, as the rest of the orchestra had done, but the First Class, his face wearing a worried frown.

Henrietta regarded him for a moment with interest before turning her gaze back to her father.

Lord Radford watched *The Boston Queen* weigh its anchor and steam slowly away.

He took off his hat and waved it until neither he nor the quayside were visible anymore.

Henrietta stayed a long while at the railing, staring out over the petrel grey sea.

America was receding into the distance. For all its attractions, she had not found love there.

Would she find love in England, she wondered.

A chill sea breeze began to blow, but that did not drive Henrietta away from the rail.

It was only when the shoreline had disappeared that she turned and went in search of her cabin.

She walked along the deck and hesitated. Had she missed the entrance to the ship's interior?

There was nothing before her here but a small white gate with 'Crew Only' written on it.

She glanced back.

The gentleman she had seen waiting anxiously on the quayside was coming along the deck towards her.

"Excuse me, sir, but is that the entrance to the First Class section over there?" asked Henrietta as he drew near.

He turned lively brown eyes upon her.

"Why, sure. But you are nearer to the starboard entrance now."

"I am?" answered Henrietta dubiously, not certain of what 'starboard' entailed.

"Yeah. Follow me."

He opened the white gate in front of them and stood aside for Henrietta to pass.

"But that says 'Crew Only'," remarked Henrietta.

The gentleman shrugged.

"So? Pretend I'm a sailor and put the blame on me. You can go round the back here and cross to the First Class deck. I have to go down to Second Class to see my troop."

"Your troop?"

"I'm the leader of the orchestra. You could have seen 'em boarding."

"Oh. Oh, yes. I did."

He smiled and held out his hand.

"Eddie Bragg's the name."

Henrietta, hesitatingly, took his hand and shook it.

"I'm Hen – Harrietta Reed," she told him shyly.

"Glad to meet you, Miss Reed."

He gestured to the open gate.

"So – you coming?"

Henrietta glanced along the deck and then passed cautiously through the white gate.

"See now, you haven't been struck by lightening," laughed Eddie.

"N-no," smiled Henrietta. "I haven't."

The breeze was stronger here and she had to clamp her hand to her hat to prevent it being torn from her head.

"Just follow the deck round," Eddie advised loudly. "You'll find a white gate and you're back in First Class."

"Thank you very much."

They shook hands again and Eddie moved away.

She watched him as he descended a twisting steel stairway, his coat flying out in the wind.

A few seconds later she noticed a flat leather folder lying at her feet.

Eddie must have been carrying it under his coat. It had probably dropped when they had shaken hands.

She picked it up quickly and followed Eddie down and found that she was now on the Second Class deck.

There was no sign of Eddie, so she moved along the deck, peering in through several glass doorways, unsure of where to find him.

She came to another white gate.

Once again it said 'Crew Only', but knowing Eddie Bragg, this would be no deterrent. She paused, opened it, and stepped through to see if he might have gone that way.

She was now looking down into what seemed to be a cargo deck at the back of the ship.

There was no cargo, but there were a large number of people. Shabbily dressed, pale and thin, they huddled together or paced the enclosed deck for warmth.

With a shock, she realised that she was looking at the Steerage section – where the poorest people travelled.

Someone began to play a mouth organ.

A gentleman shrouded in a full cloak of a material a good deal more expensive than his fellow passengers were wearing, turned away with a shrug of disgust and strode to a door at the back of the deck.

As he turned, Henrietta caught sight of a thin nose, thin as the blade of a knife –

The profile so resembled that of Prince Vasily of Rumania that Henrietta's hand flew to her mouth.

"Miss Reed? Are you all right?"

It was Eddie, standing at her elbow and regarding her with concern.

"I-I'm fine. Thank you. It's just that – I thought I recognised someone I knew."

She peered over the rail again, but the gentleman in the cloak had gone.

"Someone you knew? In Steerage?"

He sounded so surprised that she shook herself and gave a gay little laugh.

"You are right – the person I knew would never – "

Eddie's eyes twinkled.

"A *he*, eh?"

Henrietta grew flustered. Mr. Bragg's manner was more informal than she was used to from a stranger and she should by rights have been offended.

But his face was so open, his demeanour so good-humoured and thoughtful, that she did not think it right to correct him.

The world of *The Boston Queen* was so unlike any world she had ever known and besides, Eddie was an artist. He was different. And, of course, he had no idea that she was the daughter of a Lord!

"Mr. Bragg. I believe you dropped this whilst we were talking."

"Eddie, please, not Mr. Bragg. And yes, that's my music folder. Thank Heavens! I was looking for it. My latest composition could have been lost had I not found it."

Henrietta's eyes widened.

"You are a composer?"

"Yes, but alas, fair lady, I am far better known as a conductor!"

She turned and began to make her way back along the Second Class deck with Eddie at her heels.

"I cannot let you go without a promise that you'll take a cocktail with me," he insisted breezily.

"I have never drunk a cocktail in my life," replied Henrietta truthfully.

She began to climb up the stairs and again, Eddie followed her.

She hurried to the white gate that led through to the First Class area, but Eddie darted ahead and reached it first.

"Well then," he puffed, opening the gate, "I'll just have to dedicate a number for you when we play at dinner tomorrow night."

Then his face darkened.

"*If* we play – "

Henrietta was about to ask what he meant by this qualification when she caught sight of two ladies, one of whom was staring disapprovingly her way.

The elder of the two was tall and stout with a long imperious nose and a haughty expression. She was swathed in furs and a purple hat that the wind tugged at viciously.

The other one was younger, perhaps not much older than Henrietta. She was also tall, but thin as a post, with tiny boot black eyes and a nervous grimace on her face.

"I wonder how it is that the gate is not locked," said the haughty woman. "It is simply wrong that Second Class passengers should come up here without a by or leave!"

"Yes, Lady Butterclere, it is indeed," sniffed her thin companion.

Eddie seemed amused.

"If it's any of your business, Lady B-B – whatever, we're First Class passengers who decided to see how the other half lives!"

"How the other half lives?"

Lady Butterclere's voice rose to a shrill crescendo that was in direct competition with the wind.

"I have no idea why anyone should wish to do such a ridiculous thing. But if you *are* First Class, I wonder that any young lady should be without a chaperone. Unless *you* are her chaperone – a relation, perhaps?"

"Her *chaperone*?"

Eddie threw back his head and roared with laughter.

"I'm no chaperone, Lady Buttery. I'm a composer and conductor of the Eddie Bragg Orchestra."

Lady Butterclere's lip curled with distaste.

"An *artiste*."

She drew her furs closer about her as if in danger of being contaminated.

"I might have guessed."

With that, she swept away, crooking her finger at her companion to follow.

"Well," observed Eddie chuckling, "if that doesn't beat all! She must think she's become *The Boston Queen* incarnate!"

"Oh, Eddie!" expostulated Henrietta, trying so hard not to join his burst of laughter.

Eddie stared, ruminating, after the two ladies.

"You know, I'm sure I've seen that skinny Lizzie who was with her before."

"Skinny Lizzie?" repeated Henrietta, puzzled.

"That's what we call a girl who – aw, never mind. Say, now I've got my music folder back, I'd better get on down to check that the fellows have settled in. So good to meet you, Miss Reed."

"Good to meet you, Eddie," murmured Henrietta to his already retreating back.

She had never met anyone quite like Eddie Bragg.

This time she made her way without any difficulty all the way to her cabin.

Nanny had unpacked the trunk and hung everything up and now suggested that she take a nap before supper.

Lord Radford had arranged for the cabin to be filled with roses and their scent filled the air.

As Henrietta lay dreamily in her bunk, the image of the gardens at Lushwood floated before her.

It was to be longer before she saw them again than she could ever have imagined.

Nanny woke her excitedly.

"The dinner gong has sounded," she cried. "And we are invited to dine at the Captain's table!"

"We are?"

"A Steward brought the invitation on a tray. It said '*Miss Reed and Mrs. Poody are hereby requested to dine at the Captain's table this evening –* ' or something like that."

Henrietta slipped her feet over the side of her bunk.

"I wonder why we've been invited, when as far as the Captain knows we are not important or interesting."

"Well, I just don't know to be sure," replied Nanny, "but I have accepted the invitation on your behalf."

"That's all right, Nanny. It will be an adventure."

Henrietta remembered that on the voyage out, she and her father had been invited to the Captain's table, but not Nanny. Now, as the chaperone, 'Mrs. Poody,' she was to be included and Henrietta understood her delight.

"There's a grey silk gown that will be just perfect for you tonight, Nanny, and you can borrow my pearls."

She was going to enjoy it all as much as Nanny!

Heads turned as she entered the dining room.

Tendrils of blonde hair fell over her high pale brow and about her slender swan-like neck.

Her eyes gleamed like huge emeralds and were full of life as she surveyed the scene before her.

'Why,' she mused in surprise, 'there's Eddie Bragg at the Captain's table!'

Eddie rose with the Captain as they approached.

"You are most welcome, ladies," boomed out the Captain jovially.

They sat down and the Captain was soon chatting to Mrs. Poody, while Eddie leaned across to Henrietta.

"I guess you're wondering why my troop are all in Second Class while I'm in First?" he whispered.

Henrietta nodded, as she sipped a glass of water.

"Well," explained Eddie, with obvious enjoyment, "the Captain just happens to be my cousin. He's allowed the orchestra to travel at a reduced rate, but being a family member means *I* travel free, so naturally, I choose the best! The troop are a decent bunch – they don't mind if I sleep in a feather bed now and then!"

"I see, but that doesn't explain why – "

"Why you and the chaperone are here?" he finished for her. "Well, I arranged the invitation. Walter – Captain Hanket, that is to say, is always happy to have a few pretty ladies at his table."

Henrietta blushed and then glanced at two laid but empty places at the table.

Eddie followed her gaze.

"Ah, you're wondering what other pretty ladies are to join us! Well, if you could see those place cards from where you're sitting you'd realise what perfect specimens of beauty are scheduled to shine at us over the stew – Miss Romany Foss and Lady Maud *Butterclere!*"

Henrietta blenched.

"Oh, my goodness. You – you arranged for *them* to be invited too?"

Eddie chuckled.

"Heaven's, no. That was the Captain's doing. But don't worry – they sent word that they cannot attend."

"They're not coming?" she asked in palpable relief.

"No," replied Eddie with unmistakable glee. "Poor

Miss Foss has motion sickness and Lady Butterclere can't leave her side, so it leaves me with only one exquisite face to gaze on instead of three!"

He winked at Henrietta.

She lowered her eyes for she really did not know what to make of Eddie. She was never certain if he was genuinely complimenting her or merely teasing her.

Most of the time, he seemed to treat her as an equal, almost as one of his troop.

With a sudden frisson she realised that for once she was being taken exactly at her face value – someone with enough to travel First Class, but not someone attached to one of the established and aristocratic families of England.

"What are you smiling at?" asked Eddie softly.

"Smiling? Was I?"

"Oh, yes."

To her consternation, he leaned his elbows on the table and clasped his hands under his chin to gaze on her.

"You remind me of a song I wrote recently."

Softly, Eddie began to sing.

"*Your eyes sparkle, like the sun on the sea, sparkle for all men – and never just me. I can't tell who you are or what you are you – mysterious girl! But I'm here to reveal – you set my heart a-whirl.*"

Henrietta felt her cheeks flush scarlet.

In the meantime both Captain and Mrs. Poody had stopped talking to listen.

"Why that's – that's so *new world*," exclaimed Mrs. Poody at the end of the song.

"Oh, our Eddie's a real new worlder," explained the Captain pleasantly. "Even if he was born in London!"

"You were?" questioned Mrs. Poody.

"In Clapham," nodded Eddie. "My parents came out to America in 1862. I was ten at the time. My Mum's brother had already emigrated to New York."

Every so often Henrietta stole a glance at Eddie.

There was something engaging about him.

His brown hair fell over his eyes, which were warm and full of humour and he really did sing like a dream, but already he felt more like a brother to her than a suitor.

She sincerely hoped he was not going to court her, for she would never wish to wound him with a refusal.

"You will have a real treat Wednesday night, Mrs. Poody," she heard the Captain saying to Nanny, "when the Eddie Bragg Orchestra play at dinner!"

There was a long silence, while Eddie stared down at his plate. At last he looked up.

"A problem, cousin. I've lost my piano player!"

"*Lost* him?"

"He didn't make departure. I waited for him on the quayside as long as I could. Stuck in some low down bar, I wouldn't wonder. But we're in real trouble for most of the programme. It's built around the piano."

"Surely you can look for a replacement?" asked the Captain. "*Someone* on board must be able to play."

"Of course," came in Mrs. Poody, "Hen – Harrietta there is most accomplished at the keyboard."

Henrietta gazed at Nanny feeling flustered.

She wished her old nanny had not said it. She was getting so carried away with it all that she was beginning to forget that Henrietta was supposed to be Harrietta.

Eddie was now regarding her with renewed interest.

"You play?"

"She plays as good as anyone I've heard!" declared

Mrs. Poody. "She was taught by her mother and *she*, bless her, studied at the Conservatoire in Paris."

Eddie pushed back a lock of hair from his forehead.

"Can I hear you play?" he asked Henrietta urgently. "You just might be the answer. And boy, would you be easy on the eye!"

Henrietta stared at him in horror.

"I couldn't possibly," she began and then her voice trailed away as she realised her predicament.

How could she possibly explain that the daughter of Lord Radford could not be seen performing in public with any orchestra in the world – let alone with the Eddie Bragg Company of New York?

Such wayward behaviour would never be condoned in aristocratic circles!

The problem was, for the purposes of this voyage, she was not an aristocrat. She was just plain Miss Harrietta Reed and there was no protocol that she knew of to prevent a Miss Reed from playing at least for one night.

"Aw, don't be modest, just allow me to hear a few notes," pleaded Eddie, misinterpreting her confusion.

"Go on," encouraged Mrs. Poody, waving her fork at her charge. "I'm sure you would enjoy it."

Henrietta toyed with the stem of her glass.

"Well – "

"Great!"

Eddie clapped his hands.

"After dinner, when everyone has left the dining room, you can try out on the grand over there."

Turning, Henrietta could see a dais at the end of the room with a piano under a white sheet.

Now that Henrietta might prove to be the answer to

his problem, Eddie appeared to see her in a new light. A professional rather than a romantic light.

He talked enthusiastically about his plans for his orchestra, the successful tour they had just completed in major American cities and a two-month run in New York.

They were booked to play at the *Haymarket* theatre in London for a season.

"What I really hope for," he said dreamily, "is to be invited to play at all the great houses in England. Maybe even at Buckingham Palace!"

"A pity then that Lady Butterclere couldn't be with us tonight," mused the Captain. "She is the stepsister of a Duke and is on her way to take up residence on his estate."

Eddie shrugged.

"I wouldn't have thought she had a musical bone in her body."

"Maybe not, but she moves in the right circles."

"Does she live in America?" asked Mrs. Poody.

The Captain nodded.

"Seems she was widowed about twenty years ago, but was left without a bean by Lord Butterclere. So she came to America to look for a rich husband."

Henrietta lifted her head with interest.

"Only she never found one, leastwise that anyone knows of," the Captain continued.

"That anyone knows of – ?" repeated Mrs. Poody.

The Captain grunted.

"There was talk she met someone out West. But why would she accept her stepbrother's offer of a home if she had a husband? Besides, she continues to call herself 'Butterclere'.

"That she is," agreed Eddie. "But who's the poor little mouse she's travelling with?"

"That lady is no mouse, but the intended fiancée of Lady Butterclere's stepbrother, the Duke of Merebury," added Captain Hanket.

"How do you know?" demanded Mrs. Poody.

He stroked his beard with a twinkle in his eye.

"A Captain knows everything about his passengers, Mrs. Poody."

Henrietta shrank into her seat. She sincerely hoped that was not true, at least not in her case!

Eddie seemed to read her thoughts.

"Ah-ah, but he doesn't know about *you*, Miss Reed! You're the enigma that appears on every voyage."

The Captain laughed and pushed back his seat.

"I am just going to greet a few of the other diners. Then, Mrs. Poody, we'll go to the lounge for coffee. Eddie and Miss Reed have other business to attend to!"

Eddie stood up and held out his hand to Henrietta.

"Ready?"

She nodded and rose, taking his hand to be led over to the dais.

Eddie removed the white sheet from the piano.

"What're you going to play?" he asked as Henrietta sat down and ran her fingers over the keys.

She thought for a moment, her head on one side.

"A waltz," she said at last.

"Okay. Fire away."

The melody held her quickly in its grasp and she forgot all about her surroundings.

She was back at Lushwood, playing in the drawing room. The doors to the garden were open and a ray of soft sunshine fell on the carpet. Her beloved mother was there too, listening to the music with a smile on her face.

Tears welled up into Henrietta's eyes and trickled down her cheeks as she finished the piece and let her hands fall into her lap.

Eddie was silent for a moment.

"The keys sing under your fingers," he said at last.

Henrietta gently closed the lid of the piano.

"So – ?" she ventured, not knowing what response he actually desired.

"So – you'll do," responded Eddie softly.

His gaze lingered on her animated face, her pearly teeth visible between half-parted lips, her porcelain cheeks pink, her huge eyes moist with tears.

"Tomorrow I'll introduce you to the troop. They'll bleat a little at first – you being a female and all – but I'm sure they'll take to you."

"And if they don't?"

"I'll have them all flogged and thrown overboard! Now let's go and join them in the lounge. I could sure use a glass of brandy!"

As Henrietta allowed herself to take Eddie's arm, she suddenly had to stifle a giggle.

She felt light headed at the thought of who she may become within the next few days!

"*Miss Harrietta Reed, pianist and member of the Eddie Bragg Orchestra!*"

CHAPTER THREE

Henrietta frowned as she leafed through her gowns. Most of them seemed too girlish for a performer.

In the end she picked out a plain rose-coloured silk, to be matched with an ermine cape and long white gloves.

At the arranged time she entered the dining room.

Twenty pairs of eyes followed her as she walked to the dais, where Eddie was waiting for her.

She suddenly felt very shy as he gently turned her around to face the members of the orchestra, who lounged silently on their chairs below.

"Gentlemen," he announced. "Here is our saviour, Miss Harrietta Reed, *pianiste extraordinaire!*"

"That will remain to be seen," muttered one.

"Or rather heard," said another, a bald man who sat before a kettle drum.

This was just the kind of reception Henrietta had expected and her spirits sank.

"Be not of faint heart," whispered Eddie.

Henrietta sat down on the piano stool whilst Eddie positioned some music sheets before her.

"You can sight-read, I presume?" he asked.

"Of course," replied Henrietta meekly.

"I'll turn the pages. Okay. Shoot."

She laid trembling fingers on the keys and began to play.

Though her eyes were fully focused on the music displayed before her, Henrietta was still acutely aware of the critical gaze of her audience. She could not relax and soon she was stumbling over her notes.

She raised desperate eyes to Eddie and he held up his hand at once for her to stop.

"I don't think the dame is quite right for us, Eddie," called out the clarinet player.

Eddie frowned and took the music from the stand.

"I-I'm sorry," stammered Henrietta quietly.

She half rose, but Eddie waved her down again.

"Why don't you just play something you know and love, like you did last night? This stuff is new to you and needs practice. Show 'em what you can really do, huh?"

Henrietta hesitated.

"Go on," urged Eddie. "You can do it."

Henrietta thought a moment and then began to play a French air that her mother had taught her.

Her fingers fluttered lightly over the keys like birds in flight. She began to sway to the sounds that emerged melodiously from the piano.

Soon she forgot where she was – eyes closed, she was transported to a dew-drenched garden under the moon. A tall figure came forward from the shadows – the figure of a man, with aquiline features and dark, brooding eyes, his hair black as a raven's wing.

'*How strange*,' she thought dreamily. She did not recognise the gentleman at all.

The music flowed and as it neared the end, it rose into a trill of delicate notes like birdsong at dawn.

Henrietta opened her eyes on the final flourish.

She waited, head lowered, for the verdict.

"Bravo!" called a voice from the dining room floor.

Suddenly the whole of the orchestra were clapping. She looked up, astonished, and could see Eddie beaming.

"You've done it, Miss Reed," he cried.

"I-I have?"

"Sure."

He held out his hand to her.

"Welcome to the Eddie Bragg Orchestra."

"W-what happens now?" she asked.

"We rehearse!"

Henrietta spent the morning rehearsing with the rest of musicians. Now she was more confident, soon mastering the melodies for which the Eddie's orchestra was famous.

After the rehearsal finished Eddie introduced her to the individual musicians.

Trescot, the trumpeter, looked her up and down.

"That's a pretty outfit, but shouldn't she be wearing something a little more eye-catching for the performance?"

Eddie pondered.

"Miss Reed, what else have you brought with you?"

"I don't have anything more suitable than this," she confessed, looking from Trescot to Eddie helplessly.

Trescot turned to Eddie.

"My Kitty has a few colourful frocks."

"Kitty is his – er – companion," Eddie explained to Henrietta. "She's the only woman on the trip with us."

He suggested that they visit Trescot's cabin to take a look at Kitty's wardrobe.

Once again Henrietta found herself in the Second Class section of the ship.

She drew her cape over her shoulders and glanced nervously around as Trescot opened the door to his cabin.

"Kitty's here," he called over his shoulder as Eddie and Henrietta entered behind him.

A plump woman with tousled hair inspected them from her bunk. She was lying one arm under her head with her features almost hidden under wreaths of cigar smoke.

"Kitty, we've got a piano player!" Eddie told her, indicating Henrietta. "Thing is, she didn't board the ship expecting a new career, so she has nothing suitable to wear for tonight. Have you anything she could borrow?"

Kitty gestured to a trunk, which stood half open and still unpacked in the corner of the cabin.

Eddie and Trescot started pulling garments from the trunk, while Henrietta looked away as garish camisoles and bodices landed in a heap with gaudy skirts and frocks.

All the while she was aware of Kitty regarding her with lazy amusement.

"Hey, this looks possible."

Eddie now held up a deep scarlet gown with puffed sleeves and plunging neckline.

"Are – you sure?" asked Henrietta dubiously.

"Absolutely!" said Eddie cheerfully. "It will add a real touch of glamour. Why don't you try it on for size?"

"I will help her," suggested Kitty, sliding her legs over the side of the bunk, cigar in her mouth.

After Eddie and Trescot withdrew Henrietta slipped out of her dress and stepped into the scarlet gown.

"You're an unlikely find," remarked Kitty. "Purty little thing that you are. You got no protector on board?"

"Protector? Well, I have my Nan – a companion, Mrs. Poody."

"You're gonna need more than any Mrs. Poody to protect you in that!" chuckled Kitty.

"I can – protect myself well enough," said Henrietta somewhat stiffly.

Kitty took the cigar from her mouth.

"Honey, don't get mad at me. I do know the boys. They've quite an eye for a purty gal."

"E-even Eddie?" she enquired, as she was thinking of Eddie as someone she could turn to in a crisis.

"*Especially* Eddie!" giggled Kitty.

Her gaze softened as she took in Henrietta's alarm.

"Uh-oh! You haven't fallen for Eddie, have you?"

"No, I haven't!" exclaimed Henrietta truthfully.

"That's healthy of you. The only real passion in his life is music anyway."

With that she threw open the cabin door and called out down the corridor.

Eddie and Trescot whistled as they entered.

"My, oh my!" exclaimed Eddie, shaking his head. "What do you think, Trescot?"

"An eyeful, all right," chortled Trescot.

Henrietta blushed.

"I-I'm not sure. I d-don't feel like *me* in it."

"You're a *new* you, that's all. You'll need some make-up, of course."

"Make-up?" Henrietta echoed.

"I'll sort that before the performance tomorrow," offered Kitty.

"Right," declared Eddie, rubbing his hands. "Well, let's go show the others the dress, shall we?"

As the two men opened the door to usher her out, Henrietta threw a hapless look over her shoulder at Kitty.

Kitty threw herself back on the bunk and lay there, drawing on her cigar.

"Lamb to the slaughter," she murmured as the door closed behind the two men and Henrietta.

*

The following day Henrietta spent most of her time rehearsing with the orchestra. Eddie was a perfectionist and wanted to be sure there would be no mishaps.

It was late afternoon by the time Eddie consulted his watch and laid down his baton.

"Okay, we'll call it a day," he suggested. "I wonder if we should meet tomorrow to run through it all again – "

The whole orchestra – including Henrietta – let out a groan in unison.

Eddie threw up his hands.

"If you're happy, fellas, I'm happy too."

Henrietta was too exhausted to join them for dinner. She ordered food to be brought to her cabin.

Nanny stayed with her although Henrietta could see the old lady was chafing to be Mrs. Poody again.

The next evening Henrietta was feeling too nervous to attend dinner, although she and Mrs. Poody had once again been invited to dine with the Captain. She insisted that Nanny go without her, but she was reluctant.

"Oh, you should go, Nanny. The Captain will be disappointed if neither of us appears. Besides I will have to wear the dress I'm performing in at the table and I don't want to spoil the surprise!"

She felt that she could as well have said 'shock' instead of 'surprise'.

She had a feeling Nanny was not going to approve of the scarlet gown. If she appeared in it at dinner Nanny might make a fuss, but once she was at the piano her outfit was a *fait accompli*!

She remembered that Lady Butterclere and Romany Foss were likely to be guests of the Captain tonight and she shrank from revealing herself to their disapproving gaze.

Luckily Nanny was persuaded in the end to go to dinner without her.

Henrietta waited for a moment after Nanny had left before opening the door and peering along the corridor.

It had been decided that she should make her own way to Kitty's cabin, where Kitty would help her dress.

The corridor was now empty, so she slipped out and hurriedly made her way to Second Class.

"You're late," scolded Kitty as she opened the door to Henrietta. "The dinner gong rang a while ago."

"I'm not going in to dinner," she replied, stepping quickly out of her dress. "I'm not hungry."

Kitty shrugged and handed Henrietta a peignoir.

"Here, put that on while I make you up. We don't want to get lipstick on your costume, do we?"

"L-lipstick?"

Henrietta had never worn lipstick before – nor any cosmetics for that matter.

"And rouge, too," elaborated Kitty. "We are going to make you the absolute belle of the ball!"

Henrietta sat patiently as Kitty worked, whistling as she applied the powder and paint.

"You stepping out with anyone, honey?" she asked as she pressed the puff to Henrietta's cheeks.

"No, I'm not."

"And no one in mind?"

She hesitated as, for some strange reason, the image

43

of a gentleman with his aquiline features and dark brooding eyes rose in her mind. It was the same gentleman she had envisaged when she was playing the French air.

She was beginning to feel haunted by him.

She somehow associated him with her return home – as if he was waiting ahead for her in her future.

She gave herself a shake before she replied.

"No one – really."

"I'm sure there'll be someone real soon, you're just too purty – " added Kitty breezily, when there came the noise of a sudden brouhaha from the corridor outside.

Running footsteps and shouts and the sound of a scuffle. Henrietta shrank in her chair, but Kitty threw open the door to see what was happening.

"What's going on?" she asked a Steward.

He gestured towards the end of the corridor.

"That fellow over there they are restraining. He is from Steerage. He stabbed a fellow during a poker game. Tried to escape this way, but we've got him now."

"Did the other fellow die?" asked Kitty baldly.

"No, thank God, but our assailant here will have to be locked up till we sail into Liverpool. Step back, lady, they're bringing him this way."

A man, wrapped up in a cape and held on two sides by Stewards, was bundled protesting past the door.

"How dare you take hold of me – I am a *Prince*!" he cried angrily, struggling to free himself.

Henrietta froze.

That voice – was it familiar?

"D-did that man say – he was a Prince?" she asked Kitty falteringly.

"Sure, but them Princes are ten a penny these days,

Steerage is full of 'em. I sometimes go down there to dance or play cards and believe me, every second fellow is Prince of Timbuktu or something."

Her down-to-earth appraisal reassured Henrietta.

'I'm too jumpy,' she thought.

She was imagining Prince Vasily under every rug!

He *could* have found out that she was travelling on *The Boston Queen* – tongues wagged, she knew that, but what reason on earth had he to follow her?

She had made her view clear and there were plenty of other hapless heiresses to pursue in America.

Whistling, Kitty took Henrietta's chin in her hand and turned her face this way and that under the lamplight.

"That'll do," she announced with a final flourish of the powder puff.

She held up a mirror and Henrietta gave a start.

Who *was* that young lady staring back at her? The kohl around the eyes, the vivid red lips and the high pink of the cheeks, gave her a sophisticated and knowing air.

It was not Henrietta Radford, but somebody else entirely different.

'*Harrietta Reed*', she felt suddenly with a sense of mounting hysteria and began to giggle uncontrollably.

"Hey, just what's so funny? I think you look like a woman of the world!" said Kitty, stung that her handiwork was not admired.

"B-but what would my f-father say?"

"I don't know, but he's not here to say it!" rejoined Kitty. "So why worry?"

"I suppose you're right," she murmured.

She also wondered what Nanny would say, but she could hardly reveal that fear to Kitty.

45

When Henrietta first stepped onto the dais with the Eddie Bragg Orchestra, she did not dare look towards the Captain's table, where she knew Nanny was sitting – as well as Lady Butterclere and Romany Foss.

Eyes low, she sat down at the piano and listened as Eddie began to introduce himself and his orchestra. He left his most recent member to last.

When she heard him mention "*our new pianist Miss Harrietta Reed*," she was forced to turn round and nod.

In that one moment, she became aware of Nanny's thunderstruck gaze.

Eddie lifted his baton and the music began.

After a few bars it was evident that the evening was going to be a success. Henrietta could sense the tapping feet, the smiles and the muttered approval.

After the final number, the applause was prolonged and enthusiastic.

Eddie insisted on leading Henrietta to the front of the dais. Her shy curtsy was in puzzling contrast to her gaudy make-up and plunging *décolletage*.

The audience, mainly the men, responded heartily. Many stood up to extend their congratulations as Eddie led her over to the Captain's table.

Lady Butterclere looked around in alarm as Eddie drew out a seat and Henrietta sat down.

"I don't think it appropriate for us to be seated here with a – with a *performer*," she hissed at the Captain.

"No?" responded Captain Hanket jovially. "Then pray do not let me detain you, Lady Butterclere. You are welcome to find a seat elsewhere!"

She half rose and then, noting that everyone present looked relieved at the thought of her imminent departure, sank down again. She was not one to accommodate other people's desires in any way.

"My companion, Miss Foss, has a yen to see how the other half lives," she explained. "Since this is the only chance she is ever going to have of indulging her curiosity, it would be wrong to deprive her of the opportunity."

Nanny, who had been looking at Henrietta with a mixture of astonishment and dismay, now turned her stare on Lady Butterclere.

"Just who are you referring to as the *other* half?" she demanded grimly.

"Why, a certain class of character – such as that of Miss Reed and yourself, not to mention Mr. Bragg – that is alien to our own," she replied haughtily.

"Now see here – " began Mrs. Poody angrily when she was silenced by a quick look from Henrietta.

"I am sure I had no idea I was so interested in such things," murmured Miss Foss wonderingly.

"Well, you are," declared Lady Butterclere firmly.

Miss Foss's beady eyes half closed for a moment. When they reopened she seemed to have grasped what was now expected of her.

"Yes, I'd love to know what your life is like," she now addressed Henrietta. "I suppose you stay up all night in bars and smoke and drink and I daresay you've had lots of affairs with unsuitable men?"

Henrietta was dumbstruck by her question and it was Eddie who mischievously answered for her.

"She's broke many a heart twixt here and Dixie!"

Henrietta rounded on him.

"Eddie!"

Mrs. Poody rapped him on the knuckles with the sugar spoon.

"You could make trouble with remarks like that!"

Romany Foss, however, was intrigued, as her eyes roved over Henrietta's costume.

"I've broken a heart or two myself, "she admitted finally, "but I'm not going to break any more, because I'm going to be married soon in England."

"Congratulations," mumbled Henrietta.

"Who to?" asked Mrs. Poody doubtfully.

"Oh, a Duke," preened Miss Foss.

"My stepbrother, the Duke of Merebury," enlarged Lady Butterclere.

"Stepbrother?" wondered Mrs. Poody with an air of innocence. "You are not Merebury blood yourself, then?"

Lady Butterclere bridled at the implication that she herself might not be of aristocratic lineage.

"The present Duke's father died young. His mother then married Sir Archibald Gwyneth, who was a widower with one child – myself. The Gwyneths are an ancient well established family in Monmouthsire."

"Oh, I'm sure, I'm sure," nodded Mrs. Poody with a wicked smile.

"Unfortunately," carried on Lady Butterclere, "the Duke's grandfather did not approve of his daughter-in-law remarrying at all and so he cut her out of his will. Which is just why *I* never inherited anything from the Merebury fortune through my stepmother.

"And which is why I became somewhat estranged from the present Duke. He didn't live with his mother and my father, but remained with his grandfather at Merebury.

"It was only when he inherited the title three years ago that he contacted me, feeling that his late mother and I, his stepsister, had been unfairly treated. Which is certainly the case and I am delighted that he is now so well aware of his obligations towards me."

"He's awfully good-looking," simpered Miss Foss with a yearning sigh. "I've seen his photograph. He has raven-black hair and dark eyes and he's six foot tall."

As Henrietta listened intently, the *élan* induced by her success that evening drained from her, drop by drop.

A curious feeling rose in her breast – a kind of pain, insidious and unpleasant. It was a moment or two before she realised that it was *jealousy*, pure and simple.

Jealousy of Miss Foss and her raven-haired Duke.

She raised her fan and held it to her face, moving it to and fro as if to cool her burning cheeks.

She wished Miss Foss would stop her eulogy about the Duke.

"He's very rich and generous and he could have had anyone he chose – but he chose me," she continued.

"When did he propose?" asked the Captain.

Miss Foss now looked a little flustered. She threw a nervous grimace towards Lady Butterclere.

"Well, he – I haven't actually met him yet – "

Lady Butterclere's bosom heaved as she rushed to her companion's aid.

"There is an *understanding* between both of them," she said firmly.

The Captain's eyebrow rose.

"Oh, an *understanding*, eh?"

"There has been much correspondence between my stepbrother and myself on the subject of Miss Foss. I have not failed to make him fully aware of her unique qualities.

"He will very soon be able to appreciate them for himself, as we are travelling directly to Merebury Court from Liverpool. There is to be a ball held at Merebury on the next evening in honour of the Prince of Wales."

Eddie's ears pricked up immediately.

"*The Prince of Wales*?" he repeated.

"Yes, indeed. He is stopping off after a hunting expedition. I am to be the hostess for the evening."

Eddie toyed with a crust of bread thoughtfully.

"I've heard that the Prince is a great music lover."

"He loves entertainments of all sorts."

"So," enquired Eddie casually, "what have you laid on for him?"

"I beg your pardon?"

"In the way of music?"

For the first time Lady Butterclere looked a little non-plussed.

"Well, I am not certain if my stepbrother, the Duke, has considered – I certainly hadn't thought – "

"Maybe you *should* think, Lady Butterclere," added Eddie. "After all, one must please a Prince at all times.

"Now if you'll excuse me, I must congratulate my troop. They played so beautifully tonight. Pity the Prince was not here. I'm sure it would have all been to his taste!"

Hands in pockets, Eddie strolled over to the table where his players had gathered to discuss the evening.

The exchange between Eddie and Lady Butterclere had given Henrietta time to recover from the disconcerting feelings that had engulfed her as Miss Foss described the Duke of Merebury.

Now she lowered her fan and regarded Miss Foss with objective interest.

"Is it a long since you were in England?" she asked.

Miss Foss blinked.

"Oh, I have *never* been in England."

Even the Captain looked surprised.

50

"You sound like a proper English gentlewoman to me," he commented.

"She attended an excellent school for the children of English *émigrés* in Portland, Oregon," explained Lady Butterclere.

Mrs. Poody turned to Miss Foss.

"So your parents were English?"

She threw a look of such palpable consternation at Lady Butterclere that Henrietta was puzzled.

"Both her parents were indeed English, but they are dead," said Lady Butterclere quickly. "I knew them well, which is why I have taken an interest in Miss Foss and her future."

"You have been away from England a good period yourself, Lady Butterclere?" remarked the Captain.

Lady Butterclere hesitated.

"I came out to visit America after my first husband, Lord Butterclere, died," she replied at last. "I was always one for adventure. I even ventured West for a while. But all things pall. It was time for me to go back home, which is why it is so opportune that the Duke has invited me to spend my twilight years at Merebury."

The Captain coughed and raised his glass.

"Well – here's to your new life. And here's also to the wedding of the Duke and Miss Foss. Which I have no doubt will take place if *you* are all in favour of it, Lady Butterclere."

"Oh, I am, I am," insisted Lady Butterclere in an ominous tone. "Make no mistake about it. Now, Captain, I wonder if you would be so kind as to allow me to send a wire to my stepbrother? I should like to discover whether he has employed the services of musicians for the ball."

The Captain readily agreed and led her away to his office with Romany Foss in tow.

Mrs. Poody rounded on Henrietta.

"Have you any idea of how you look?"

"Yes. Ghastly," muttered Henrietta absently.

At the Captain's toast to the forthcoming wedding that unpleasant emotion had once again swept through her.

'What is the matter with you, Henrietta? You have never even seen the Duke of Merebury!' she mused.

Seeing Henrietta look so pale and unhappy, Nanny decided to say no more on the subject of her performance – after all, it was a once in a lifetime occurrence.

Henrietta went to Kitty's cabin to return the scarlet gown and as she was returning she stopped at the rail.

The moonlight on the sea made it gleam like silver fish scales and the stars in the sky were like diamond pins.

Henrietta sighed.

It was so romantic, but she had no one to dream of.

Only a phantom, a face that flitted in and out of her consciousness and that she somehow connected now with the one man in the world she would probably never meet – the Duke of Merebury.

"A dollar for your dreams," whispered a voice.

It was Eddie.

"They're not worth a dollar."

Eddie threw back his head with a laugh.

"I can't believe that, Miss Reed! But you do seem to need cheering up and I think I have just the news for you. Believe it or not, Lady Butterclere has invited us to perform at Merebury Court the day after tomorrow. You will agree to play with us, won't you?"

Stunned, Henrietta stared at the shining water.

Merebury Court! An opportunity to set eyes on the Duke himself. It was too tempting and yet – and yet it was impossible.

Apart from that, she just simply could not perform in public again. *The Boston Queen* was one thing, England was quite another.

"I'm so sorry, Eddie – I can't," she murmured sadly and turned away.

Eddie caught her arm.

"Please, Harrietta," he pleaded. "You made such a difference tonight on the piano."

"But surely your regular player will have caught the next ship after this one? He'll be docking in Liverpool just a day after us. Plenty of time to join you at Merebury."

"That's just the point, the Captain told me that soon after we left Boston, a big storm blew up and all sea traffic is suspended for the duration.

"Louie, my pianist, can never make it in time. So you see – you gotta say *yes*!"

"It's not possible – you don't understand."

"Then tell me."

She hesitated. At least if she told him the truth he would realise how impossible it was for her to risk being recognised. Why, she had even met the Prince of Wales once with her parents!

She sat down on a bench and told her story.

At the end of it Eddie gave a whistle.

"What a tale!"

"Isn't it," she agreed, rising. "So you do see, don't you, that I can't join you at Merebury."

"I see nothing of the sort!" cried Eddie, jumping up after her. "The Duke won't have met you, so that doesn't matter. And at the ball, you won't look like yourself at all. You hardly look like yourself now but we'll go one further.

"I have a friend who's a great make-up artist. He works at the *Drury Lane* theatre. I'll wire him to come to Merebury. He'll disguise you so well, your own father wouldn't recognise you."

"Eddie, I really can't," began Henrietta, but Eddie caught her hands between his own and gazed into her eyes.

"You cannot refuse Eddie," he said. "If you refuse me, I'll go tell everyone on this ship who you really are."

Henrietta was horrified.

"Eddie, that would be a – "

"A real low-down trick?" chuckled Eddie. "Sure it would. But I want the Prince of Wales to hear my music at its best. And when it comes to my music, I am so ruthless. Surely you knew that all along?"

"Yes, Eddie, I did."

"Then you'll play?"

Henrietta, thinking of the shame of her true identity being publicly exposed, took a deep breath.

"*Yes*, Eddie, I will."

Eddie raised her hand to his lips with a wry smile.

She stared over his head at the sea, which seemed as calm and cold as a glacier.

There was no way out of it.

Miss Harrietta Reed, pianist, would be making one last appearance with the Eddie Bragg orchestra!

CHAPTER FOUR

Nanny listened in dismay to Henrietta's idea that they accompany the orchestra to Merebury.

"We should be on the train to London," she wailed. "We could be home in Lushwood by tomorrow night."

"But I-I promised Eddie I would help him this one last time," cried Henrietta desperately.

She did not dare tell Nanny about Eddie's threat of blackmail or her own uneasy desire to meet the Duke.

"Suppose there was someone at this Merebury ball who recognised you," persisted Nanny. "Have you thought of the *hignomy*?"

Henrietta stared at her until she realised what the old lady meant by that last word.

"There won't be any ignominy, Nanny. Nobody, not even you, would recognise me by the time Eddie and his make-up artist have finished with me."

"I recognised you alright in that scandalous dress you wore. If you were found out you'd never find yourself a husband – not the one you'd want, anyway."

'I think I know the one I want,' came the rush of words through Henrietta's mind.

She had had so many suitors and wanted none of them. Now she was to meet the one man in the world she was strangely convinced she could love and – and he was beyond her forever.

He was more or less engaged to another and even if

he had not been, he was most unlikely to be interested in her alter ego Harrietta Reed, piano player with a somewhat *risqué* New York orchestra.

Behind her Nanny continued grumbling.

"Your father left you in my tender care and I have already let you do more than I should!"

"You said you were proud of my piano playing."

"I was," Nanny acceded. "But how am I going to be Mrs. Poody with people of real quality about!"

Henrietta gave her a quick hug.

"But you are *real* quality, too, Nanny!"

"Go on with you!" growled Nanny.

It was to be the turning point in the discussion and a short time later Nanny agreed to go to Merebury Court.

"But only one more performance, mind!"

"Promise!" said Henrietta with the utmost sincerity.

She had no wish to stay there for too long, as she had no desire to witness the courtship of Romany Foss and the Duke develop under her very eyes.

*

The following morning a mist rose out of the sea and settled like a shroud over *The Boston Queen*.

When Henrietta took a stroll on deck after breakfast she could hardly see anything in front of her and the ship seemed almost becalmed.

She sighed and gazed into the mist.

Not far ahead lay England.

England and the Duke, with whom she was already half in love.

She felt as if she was sailing towards her destiny.

She turned as she heard footsteps approach.

"Who's – there?" someone called out nervously.

A hand reached out of the mist, groping at the air as if for support. Romany Foss stumbled after it and she gave a little shriek of relief when she saw Henrietta.

"Thank goodness! I heard someone coming and I thought supposing it's that murderer from Steerage!"

"It was unlikely to be him. He's locked up and the man he stabbed didn't die, so he's not quite a murderer."

Romany looked about her with a shudder.

"I shall be so very pleased to reach the sanctuary of Merebury Court," she sighed. "I hear you are going to be there too with the orchestra."

"That's right."

"Of course, you will excuse me for not mingling with you once we arrive. Lady Butterclere has told me that it would not be seemly."

Henrietta blinked and turned away.

"You must follow the dictates of Lady Butterclere!"

She did not add that she had no desire whatsoever to mingle with Romany at Merebury or anywhere else.

One reason was her simple desire not to be found out. It was fortuitous that her own social circle was far away from the North of England and Merebury.

She dreaded going to an event as Henrietta Radford and meeting with Lady Butterclere or Romany, who would recognise her as the Eddie Bragg pianist in an instant.

Another reason was Romany's character.

She affected a certain naivety and was in thrall to Lady Butterclere, but Henrietta could detect an ambition, a greed in her black button eyes that was disconcerting.

Romany Foss, she sensed, was the sort of girl who always got what she wanted in the end.

That she wanted the Duke of Merebury was beyond question.

She was distracted from these unpleasant reveries by the sound of the fog-horn. Its loud bellow shattered the sense of dead calm that lay about the ship.

Voices called out playfully through the mist.

"Land ahoy! England ahead."

Henrietta's heart gave a great leap.

With no more thoughts of Romany, she turned and hurried down to the cabin, where Nanny had been packing since breakfast.

*

She and Nanny watched while three gangways were lowered down to the quayside and trunks were swung out to be caught by dockworkers on shore.

A black covered wagon drew up at the foot of the gangway from Steerage and two Police Officers emerged. They strode up the gangway and disappeared from view.

Henrietta leaned over the rail.

A few minutes later the two Officers reappeared on the gangway leading a figure hunched in a dark cape.

A murmur arose around Henrietta.

"That's the blaggard that tried to murder someone on board!"

The felon clearly did not wish his face to be seen. His hat was pulled low and he kept his eyes on the ground.

Henrietta gazed at him as he was bundled roughly into the wagon. She almost felt sorry for him.

It would be a long time before he saw England!

England!

Her heart sang as she lifted her head and looked at the shoreline.

To many it would seem so chill and cheerless that morning, but to her it was almost magical.

Mist swirled about glistening roofs, pinnacles and spires. A coppery sun, like an old English farthing, peered through pearly grey clouds. To the South and to the North, dark mountains loomed.

Directly ahead to the East lay Merebury Court.

Lady Butterclere and Miss Foss were descending the gangway and Nanny tapped Henrietta on the elbow.

"Better keep close to those two," she warned, "as we're travelling on with them."

A number of vehicles from Merebury Court stood waiting on the quayside.

Lady Butterclere and Romany Foss rode in the first carriage with the family crest on its side.

Henrietta, Nanny and Eddie were assigned a second carriage, smaller, but also sporting the Merebury crest.

A selection of old barouches, gigs and broughams, many obviously dragged out of dusty retirement, conveyed the rest of the orchestra, including the indomitable Kitty.

Eddie sat with his legs crossed, whistling under his breath. That he had practically blackmailed Henrietta into coming with him did not seem to weigh on his conscience.

Henrietta wanted to censure him, but she could not. He was just so irrepressibly cheerful and so openly blatant in his passion for music that she had to forgive him.

Besides, and this was something she hated to admit to herself, Eddie was the instrument that would allow her at least to set eyes on the Duke of Merebury, to see him and at least understand *why* he was haunting her.

"You know, I still haven't figured it all out," said Eddie, uncrossing and re-crossing his legs.

"What haven't you figured out?" asked Henrietta.

"That skinny Lizzie, Miss Foss, I'm so certain I've seen her somewhere before."

Henrietta waited, but Eddie shook his head.

"Nope. I can't place it. But it wasn't New York. It must have been somewhere out West."

Henrietta settled back against the plush upholstery, her eyes turning to the window and the unfolding scene.

Field after dank field, small cottages, a face raised here and there at the passing of this odd procession.

Nanny was already asleep and now Henrietta's own eyes began to close, lulled as she was by the steady clop of hooves and rattle of wheels on the road beneath.

She slept and dreamed.

The Duke of Merebury held out his hand and drew her to dance to the strain of the Eddie Bragg Orchestra.

She was in his arms and yet at the same time she was at the piano looking on, dressed in garish colours, her lips as red as new spilled blood –

Henrietta started up with a cry.

The carriage lurched to a halt and Nanny had been thrown against her shoulder.

From the road came sounds of shouts and whistles.

Eddie sprang to his feet and threw open the door.

"I'll see what's going on," he said and jumped out.

"Dearie me," moaned Nanny. "An accident?"

Eddie returned in a few minutes.

"Something of a drama," he reported. "A criminal has escaped the clutches of the law!"

"W-which criminal?" asked Henrietta faintly.

Eddie glanced at her.

"That fellow from the ship, who tried to stab a card

player in a poker game. He was in the back of the Police wagon with just one guard.

"Seems he had a weapon – a penknife or something – secreted in his boot. He managed to overcome the guard and get away. Threw himself off the moving vehicle, but escaped unhurt."

"Will we be held up long?" asked Henrietta.

"Not if Lady Butterclere has anything to do with it," chuckled Eddie. "She's even insisting the Police move their wagon to the side of the road so that she can proceed. I better go and let the troop know what's happening."

Henrietta and Nanny sat in silence, listening to the rain drum on the roof.

It seemed like an age before they started moving again.

"Hey, wait for me!" cried Eddie, wrenching open the door and scrambling up as the coach jolted into action.

As the procession wound its way deeper into the drenched countryside, no one on the wayside stopped to look carefully at the last vehicle of all.

There, wedged between the back of the coach and an unwieldy trunk, was the dripping figure of a man.

Hat low on his forehead, cape wrapped around his face, he hid from his pursuers and the world, the steel hilt of a knife gleaming at the top of his boot.

*

It was mid-afternoon before the first of the coaches rumbled through the gates of Merebury Court.

Henrietta leaned from the carriage window in awe.

Two miles of stately elms led up to the house and when she glimpsed it, she drew in her breath.

The grandiose façade of stone boasted hundreds of windows and the house rose to three storeys and a grand stairway swept up on two sides to the imposing entrance.

61

The door was opened at their approach and a butler appeared, flanked by the housekeeper and a footman.

The footman descended and opened the door of the first carriage and Lady Butterclere stepped out.

"The Duke is not here to greet us?" she demanded of the butler.

"He has been detained with the Prince of Wales at Buxton," he replied. "He has left instructions that you are to consider yourself at home."

"Well, I do, although," she replied, "I am somewhat disappointed that the Duke could not forsake the Prince to welcome his long-lost relation back home."

The butler did not blink.

"One cannot forsake a Prince, my Lady."

"Let's hope he makes it home for tomorrow's ball," she sniffed.

Lady Butterclere pursed her lips and, turning to the stairs, beckoned Miss Foss to follow her.

Miss Romany Foss, her neck stretched out like a stork, ascended the stairs, her beady little eyes flying hither and thither with an avaricious gleam.

Henrietta had overheard the exchange between the butler and Lady Butterclere, and felt her heart sink as she realised she must wait another day to set eyes on the Duke.

"You will see that our musical guests are settled in their quarters," called Lady Butterclere in an after-thought. "Are they to be housed over the stables?"

The butler blinked as he looked up at her.

"They are in the North wing, my Lady"

"In the house, you mean?"

Lady Butterclere froze.

"Orders of His Grace, my Lady."

She turned round and sailed into the hall with Miss Foss slithering in her wake.

Eddie handed first Nanny out of the coach and then Henrietta. Next he sauntered up the steps, cape slung over his shoulder.

"Gee, it's a Palace," Henrietta heard Kitty declare as she climbed out of her rickety barouche.

Henrietta was suddenly very pleased that Eddie and Kitty and the orchestra were here.

They provided a welcome antidote to the snobbery of Lady Butterclere and her *protégée*.

Servants had appeared and were already unloading the luggage from the various carriages.

"Hello, what's this?" a servant in britches called.

He was holding a damp and battered hat.

"It was behind this trunk," he added. "Was one of you lot riding on the back of the coach?"

All the members of the orchestra shook their heads. Kitty took the hat and examined it.

"I've not seen it before," she commented.

"Maybe you had a stowaway," grunted the servant, returning to his task of hauling the trunks down.

Kitty's eye met Henrietta's – they were thinking the same thing – suppose it was the prisoner who had escaped some miles back on their journey?

"Well, if you did have a stowaway, he's dropped off like a leech, probably got to the next town by now."

Reassured, Henrietta continued on her way.

The first sight that met her eyes as she stepped into the hall was a series of portraits lining the walls.

The nine Dukes of Merebury.

'*There he is,*' she thought with a flutter as her eyes settled on the last portrait to the right.

The wonder of it was that he so closely resembled her fantasy – the jet-black hair, the dark brooding gaze and the finely chiselled features.

He seemed to be looking directly at Henrietta. She almost blushed under that serious searching stare.

She and Nanny were shown into adjoining rooms. They were to share their bathroom, but even so Henrietta considered their quarters luxurious in the extreme.

Her four-poster was so high that steps were needed and thick gold drapes hung from the canopy.

There was a bright fire blazing in the grate.

She thought she would be tired after the long coach ride, but when she lay down for a nap, her eyes would not close.

She lay staring up at the underside of the canopy.

She imagined the Duke approaching her and, since she had seen ardour, feigned or otherwise, on the faces of her various suitors, she was now able to envisage ardour on the face of this most favoured suitor.

Her fingers traced her own lips as she imagined the kiss that the Duke might bestow upon them –

"*What are you thinking,*" she cried aloud in horror, springing up from the bed.

Running across to the dressing table, she now faced herself in the mirror.

'*You do not know the Duke and he does not know you,*' she told herself sternly. '*He is just a fantasy.*'

A fantasy that had grown steadily in proportion to the diminishing distance between America and England.

How her imagination had managed to form such a near likeness to the real man, she could not fathom.

Perhaps she had seen a photograph of him in the past, in one of the English newspapers sent out regularly to her father so that he could keep up with the news.

Yes, she thought in sudden triumph, that must be it!

She had seen his photograph at some Society event or other and his vivid image had lodged in her brain.

Such intimacy with his image, however, gave her no rights at all concerning the actual Duke.

She was in too much turmoil to sleep and glanced over at the window. Although it could only be around four o'clock, it was still winter and the light was fading already.

She wondered if she might wander out and take a stroll in the gardens.

She went to her door, opened it and peeped out. All was quiet. The travellers would be weary and ensconced in their rooms until supper.

She was sure that no one would see her and was not sure that it mattered if they did.

Since the trunks were not yet unpacked there was no coat or cloak for Henrietta, so she then tiptoed into Nanny's room and looked around.

Mrs. Poody had been given sumptuous quarters as well and no doubt she was thrilled.

Nanny's shawl lay on the bed where she was at this very moment snoring valiantly away.

Henrietta bent low, gently picked up her shawl and slipped quietly out of the room.

She did not want to go out by the front door and so she turned left in the corridor instead of right. Her instincts were correct and she found herself at the top of a flight of narrow steps that led, she guessed, to the back of the house.

At the bottom of the steps there was a stone-flagged

corridor. Loud voices and the rattle of utensils alerted her to the fact that the kitchen was nearby. She hurried past a silver room and hesitated before a large nail-studded door.

Glancing behind her, she pushed the door open and emerged into a cobbled courtyard with an archway.

She was just starting towards the archway when she was arrested by the clatter of hooves behind her.

A horse and rider swept into the courtyard. Barely had the horse halted than the rider leaped from the saddle.

He gave his horse a reassuring pat on the neck and then stood drawing off his gloves.

In the deepening shadows Henrietta could not make out his features, which were hidden under his hat.

He was tall and somewhat dishevelled, as if he had ridden at full pelt over very rough ground. His boots were muddy and his breeches were spattered all over.

He took off his hat to wipe his brow with the back of his hand and Henrietta glimpsed his muddy face.

It was obvious that he was a groom who was late returning from some errand he had been sent on.

Tossing damp strands of hair back from his eyes, the groom clamped his hat back on and turned to his horse.

He led the horse to the stone trough, but it was dry. Shaking his head, he looked round the courtyard.

"Where's that boy – " he began and then his eyes alighted on Henrietta.

"Ah, you'll do," he called. "Will you please hold my horse for a moment while I fetch him some water?"

Despite his status as groom, he had such command that Henrietta instantly obeyed.

She stepped forward and took the reins. The horse turned its head and nuzzled her waist.

"Aha!" he laughed. "Mercy the laundry maid gives him sugar, so he thinks anyone in a dress will do."

He stalked away towards the stables.

Henrietta wondered at the assurance of his gait, as if he was lord not only of the stables but also of the whole courtyard.

It was too late to walk out now, thought Henrietta. She put her hand up and stroked the horse entrusted to her.

It was a grey with a proud fierce eye – obviously a thoroughbred and she wondered that the groom had been allowed to ride him.

The groom was returning, his boots almost striking sparks from the cobbles.

Water slopped from the large bucket he carried, but he did not seem to care. He deposited the bucket on the ground and the horse lowered his head eagerly.

Henrietta and he stood silently as the horse drank.

"He was thirsty," said the groom as his steed at last lifted its head from the bucket.

"No wonder," remarked Henrietta a little tartly, "it seems you rode him too hard."

The groom regarded her from under the brim of his hat. It was too dark for Henrietta to read his expression but she detected amusement in his voice when he replied,

"*Over hill and dale, through wood and vale,*" he intoned, "*for many a weary mile.* But in my defence, I know this noble creature well and there's nothing he enjoys more than a long and challenging gallop."

"Is he – the Duke's horse?" she asked carefully.

There was a pause before the groom replied, again in an amused tone.

"He is."

"But you – exercise him?"

Another pause.

"No one but I."

"And the Duke – is he – a good Master?"

The groom lifted his hat and scratched his head as if in deliberation.

"Well now," he said slowly, "he has been known to whip the cook if the pastry is too tough, but other than that there are no complaints."

"*Whip the cook*?" repeated Henrietta in horror.

Was she about to be thoroughly disillusioned with regard to the character of the Duke?

The groom registered her dismay and gave a laugh.

"Don't let me discourage you from applying for a post at Merebury, if that's why you're here. It's a generally happy environment and the servants rarely leave."

Henrietta drew herself up, somewhat piqued that she should be mistaken for someone seeking employment at Merebury. She had forgotten that she was wearing Nanny's distinctly old and tattered shawl.

"I'm not seeking work," she retorted a little stiffly. "I am a guest of the Duke."

The toss of her head that accompanied these words dislodged the shawl – it slipped to reveal her blushing face.

The groom stared a second and then gave a whistle.

"A guest, eh? Lucky Duke, to have such a pretty visitor all to himself."

Henrietta blushed a deeper red.

"Oh, I'm not the only guest," she admitted quickly.

"You're not?" responded the groom softly, his eyes lingering on her features, seeming to drink them in. "No, of course not. You didn't travel all this way alone."

"Indeed not. There are – lots of us."

"*Lots* of us?"

"The orchestra."

She heard him sharply draw in a breath. He seemed disconcerted for a moment and then he breathed out.

"I see. So you are not – ?"

Henrietta regarded him questioningly.

"Not – who?"

The groom hesitated, then turned away and began to loosen the horse's bridle.

"No great matter. It's just I thought you might be another young lady that the Duke is expecting."

'*He means Romany Foss*,' thought Henrietta with a plunge in her heart.

She put out her hand to the horse, finding comfort in the velvety flesh of his neck.

"Well, I'm Hen – Harrietta Reed, and the Duke was not expecting *me* at all."

"No?" murmured the groom.

Henrietta waited to see if the groom would divulge his name, but it was not forthcoming so she decided to ask.

"Sir – we have spoken for some minutes and I do not know what name you go by."

"Me? Oh, I'm – er – Joe. Now if you'll excuse me, Miss Reed, I must get Gawain to his stable."

"Gawain," whispered Henrietta.

He heard her and hesitated.

"You – like horses?"

"Yes. But I have not ridden in a long while."

He seemed to consider carefully before he spoke.

"Well, perhaps I might be allowed to remedy that.

Would you like to ride out early tomorrow?"

Henrietta drew in her breath.

"Yes, oh, yes. I would. Only – "

"Only what?" Joe asked her gently.

"Only – would the Duke approve?"

Joe looked at her gravely.

"The Duke would be delighted. Come at seven in the morning and I shall make sure there is a mount saddled and waiting for you."

Turning then on his heel, Joe strode off towards the stables, Gawain lifting his head high as he trotted behind.

Henrietta watched for a moment and then turned back to the house.

For some reason, she felt suddenly elated by this encounter.

Whatever else might happen, she had made a kind of contact with the Duke.

Even if it was just with his groom and a grey horse!

CHAPTER FIVE

Nanny was awake and was groping for her shawl as Henrietta slipped into her room.

The old lady did not seem to notice Henrietta take the shawl from her own shoulders before handing it over.

"Have you ever seen such luxury as this?" Nanny asked her excitedly. "No wonder that Lady Butterclere has such airs, if she's to be hostess here. And no wonder that Miss Foss is so determined to marry the Duke."

Henrietta made no reply and her elation began to evaporate at Nanny's words.

Her heart sank so heavily every time she thought of the Duke wooing Miss Foss that she was now beginning to wonder if she had pursued the right course in agreeing to come to Merebury.

She had wanted to set eyes on the Duke if only to assuage her burning curiosity about him, but already she felt too much pain whenever her thoughts strayed his way.

There was a rumble of wheels below her window and someone called out a bold "hallooo!"

Henrietta looked out.

Three or four figures, holding lanterns aloft, were gathered around a wagon. Another figure was unhitching the two cart horses while yet another had leaped onto the wagon and was pushing a large trunk to the edge.

"Tom, take the other end of this!" called the figure on the wagon.

Tom obliged and between them they hoisted the trunk to the ground.

"Beyond me why the Duke needed so much for just a week away," panted Tom taking out a large kerchief.

"He's a Duke, Tom," cried the man on the wagon. "And he's been suppin' with the Prince of Wales for seven days. He needs more than a pair of garters to do that!"

Henrietta drew back from the window, trembling.

The Duke's luggage had returned. The Duke must be close behind, although she could not understand why his luggage had not travelled with him in his coach.

"What's all that commotion below?" asked Nanny.

"It's the Duke's luggage," explained Henrietta.

"Oh," said Nanny with interest. "Does that mean he's on his way back tonight and not tomorrow? Will we see him at supper, I wonder? My goodness me, what am I going to wear, Henrietta? Oh, what a worry all this is. I shall be glad to get back to just being myself, that I will! It's all very well playing the lady, but it's a strain!"

'I shall be very glad to get back to being my real self, too,' thought Henrietta as Nanny prattled on.

She and Nanny could easily have taken the train to London leaving Harrietta Reed and Mrs. Poody to vanish with the sea mist.

But no, here they both were, still characters in this strange shadow play – a play in which her foolish romantic heart might be well and truly broken.

"Nanny, I have absolutely the right dress for you, but it's in my trunk," answered Henrietta at last.

"You're very good to old Mrs. Poody. I hope you achieve your heart's desire one day, for you deserve it."

Henrietta smiled wanly as she patted Nanny's hand.

Her heart's desire! That was something she was never going to have!

She wandered back to her own room where a maid was busy unpacking one of her trunks.

"You are with the orchestra, miss?" asked the maid.

"Why – yes, I am," replied Henrietta faintly.

The maid closed the trunk and turned for the door.

"Oh, by the way, miss. I nearly forgot. There's a note for you, miss. There, on the dressing table."

"A note? For me?" echoed Henrietta, but the maid was gone.

The note lay on a silver platter and was sealed with the Merebury crest.

Was it some order from Lady Butterclere, flexing her muscles of authority as soon as she might?

She broke off the seal and unfolded the paper.

"*The Duke invites you to take tea with him in the library at five o'clock.*"

Henrietta blinked in disbelief and read again.

"*The Duke invites you to take tea –* "

He must have arrived before his luggage, then!

"*The Duke invites you –* "

She clasped the note to her beating breast, almost giddy as the blood thrilled in her veins.

The Duke! *She was going to meet the Duke at last*!

The chime of a distant clock broke in on her reverie and a cry of alarm escaped her lips.

A quarter to the hour!

She was going to be late.

Her mind in a whirl, she ran into Nanny's room to ask if Mrs. Poody had also been invited to tea as well, but there was no sign of the old lady.

Racing back to her own room she began to struggle out of her travelling gown.

She supposed the rest of the orchestra were invited too and hoped to catch Kitty before she left so that the two of them could go down together.

She grabbed the deep blue dress she had bought in Boston, stepped into it and as she did so she caught sight of herself in the pier glass.

Her cheeks were flushed and blonde curls strayed over her brow, but there was no time to powder her face or fix her hair.

She would be late – *late*!

She thrust her arms into the sleeves and then froze.

Who would hook it up for her? It was too late to ring for the maid.

Then she thought of Kitty.

She hastened to the room where Kitty was lodged.

Kitty looked up in astonishment as Henrietta rushed in, barely knocking to announce herself.

"What's up, honey?"

Kitty was lolling on a chair, still in a loose peignoir and painting her nails.

"Y-you won't be ready!" she cried incredulously.

"Ready for what?"

"Why, tea with the Duke."

"Honey, what makes you think I'm taking tea with the Duke?"

"Well, I-I received an invitation and I-I thought we all had."

"Not Kitty," was the amused reply.

"Oh."

Was she alone summoned then?

Greatly confused, she backed out of the room.

At the door she then wheeled around and took to her heels.

Her feet twinkled under her as she heard the clock chime, louder now and nearer the hour of five.

She was flying down the great staircase when an all too familiar voice brought her to an instant halt.

"Stop at once, young lady. Just where do you think you are going?"

Lady Butterclere stood rigid at the top of the stairs, gazing furiously down. Romany Foss lurked behind, her lips twitching with some secret amusement.

"I-I'm on my way to the library – for tea with the D-Duke," stammered Henrietta.

Lady Butterclere descended the stairs in a vapour of wrath.

"I have been given *carte blanche* by the Duke to exert my authority throughout this house," she thundered, her eyes black as billiard cues. "And believe me, I will. I *order* you this instant to return to your room."

"B-but I – can't. It is the Duke – himself who has summoned me," stammered Henrietta. "L-look."

Lady Butterclere now snatched the note from her outstretched hand and examined it through her lorgnettes.

"There has been a mistake," she said coldly. "This invitation was obviously intended for Romany."

"B-but it was delivered to *my* room."

"There has been a mistake, I tell you," she hissed, thrusting the invitation at Romany, who took it greedily.

"It's obviously meant for me," smirked Romany as she stuffed it into her bodice. "I mean, why on earth should the Duke want to take tea with a mere piano player, eh?"

Henrietta lowered her eyes unhappily.

"I-I don't know," she confessed.

"Go on, Romany." Lady Butterclere waved at her *protégée*. "The Duke is waiting."

Henrietta stared miserably at the hem of Romany's dark green skirt as it trailed on past her down the stairs.

As soon as Romany was well out of earshot, Lady Butterclere leaned menacingly towards Henrietta.

"Now you just take heed, Miss Reed. I know your sort only too well. You intercepted that note. You aim to set your cap at the Duke and distract him from Romany."

"I c-can assure you, such a thought was n-never on my mind."

"Was it not?" asked Lady Butterclere sarcastically. "Then would you explain to me why you were on your way to see the Duke *in that provocative condition*?"

For a moment, she was horribly confused. What did Lady Butterclere mean *in that provocative condition*?

With dawning horror, she remembered that she had not been able to hook up her dress – she had rushed out of Kitty's room without asking for help.

Now she glanced into the mirror on the stairs and almost burst into tears at the sight that met her eyes.

Her hair had come loose and now fell over her face untidily. Her dress had slipped off, exposing an alabaster shoulder and the tip of a heaving breast.

What was more, she had forgotten to put on any stockings or shoes and was standing there in her bare feet.

"Oh. Oh. Oh," she cried.

"I should think so too," said Lady Butterclere with grim satisfaction. "You look like a – *a common harlot*!"

Henrietta turned to stumble away and as she did so she noticed Lady Butterclere's demeanour rapidly change.

76

The woman's lips now puckered into a tight little smile as she and her skirts sank in an obsequious curtsy.

"Your Grace," she twittered.

Henrietta understood in an instant. *He* was there, the Duke, somewhere in the hall below gazing up.

Gazing up at her and her unhooked dress with her corset and slim white back exposed to all and sundry.

'Oh,' she cried again, before taking to her heels.

Back in her room she flung herself into a chair and buried her face in her hands.

She had never felt so foolish and so humiliated.

She had welcomed Eddie's ploy to get her here.

She had felt very drawn to Merebury, drawn to its handsome, raven-haired Master. He would meet her as a social inferior, but at least she would set eyes on him.

At least she would know if this burgeoning passion was more than a mere surge of emotion.

All was now lost.

The Duke himself had witnessed her confrontation with Lady Butterclere. He had seen her in *that* condition upon the stairs and heard her called 'a common harlot'.

She must perform with the orchestra as promised, but there was no way that she could be presented to him at supper or anywhere else.

It was all over for her.

Never, not in a million years could Harrietta Reed – or Henrietta Radford, for that matter, meet the handsome Duke of Merebury face to face.

*

Eddie Bragg perched on the edge of the armchair in Henrietta's room and poured himself a glass of wine.

"That Duke keeps a good cellar," he pronounced.

Kitty, lounging on the window seat, gave a snort.

"I don't expect he ever supposed half of it would end up wetting Eddie Bragg's whistle!"

Henrietta listened dully. Her visitors had dropped in after supper, wondering why she had not attended.

The Duke himself had commented on the fact that not all the orchestra were present, but Lady Butterclere had commented snootily that nobody *special* was missing.

"I'd like to have beaten her about the head with my salmon," muttered Eddie.

"She's surely got it in for you, honey," said Kitty, turning to look at Henrietta where she sat on the bed in her nightdress, knees under her chin.

"Yeah," agreed Eddie, staring at the ceiling. "And boy, does the old gorgon eat. She put away half a pound of mackerel, four lamb chops, a side of ham and a duck! That skinny Lizzie shovelled it in too! I'm sure the Duke was shocked, but he didn't show it."

"Hmn," mumbled Kitty as she looked at Henrietta more closely. "Honey, are you feeling ill? Do you need food? You don't look too great."

Henrietta, pale, her eyes red-rimmed and swollen, shook her head.

"I'm not hungry and I'm not ill. I'm just – tired."

She was praying for her visitors to go.

Kitty slid off the window seat.

"Oh, ho, I can take a hint," she whistled at Eddie. "Come on. We gotta let Harrietta here get her beauty sleep for tomorrow."

Henrietta waited until their voices faded along the corridor. Then she turned down the wick of her bedside lamp and slipped under the covers.

She longed for sleep and the ending of her troubled thoughts, but sleep did not come. She tossed and turned, imagining herself half naked under the Duke's gaze.

For that was just how she must have looked on the stairs – half naked!

Ha ha ha harlot, ha ha ha harlot.

Even the owl outside seemed to be taunting her.

The moon rose, an icy face in the dark heavens.

Henrietta at last slept, a crease on her brow.

*

When she awoke, it was to the sound of a horse stepping carefully over cobbles.

The room was light and a bird chirped on the sill.

She climbed out of bed and crossed to the window.

A chestnut mare stood saddled in the courtyard.

She pressed her forehead against the glass, staring. Was this the horse the groom had promised her?

After a moment, she turned and dressed quietly and tiptoed into the next room to find Nanny awake but in poor humour, suffering the effects of more wine than her wont.

The courtyard was silent and empty.

The mare turned her head at Henrietta's approach. She took the reins and then softly stroked the mare's nose.

"Do I have you all to myself?" she marvelled.

"Not quite," came a voice from behind.

It was Joe, his hat jammed low on his head and his face swathed in a great scarf against the frosty dawn.

"I hope you do not mind if I accompany you on the ride, Miss Reed?"

"I would be delighted," rejoined Henrietta. "To tell you the truth, I was feeling nervous at the idea of setting out alone, for I am not acquainted with the terrain."

Joe stepped forward to help her into the saddle, but held back when she was determined to mount by herself.

He looked rather startled as she settled herself with legs akimbo, her skirt trailing on either side of the mare.

Henrietta noticed his gaze and flushed.

She had forgotten the English customs of riding. In Texas she had ridden bareback, skirt hiked up into her belt.

"This is how I rode – in Texas," she explained.

How very glad she was that the Duke was not there to see her once again behaving in a questionable manner!

Joe bowed his head, seeming amused, and mounted Gawain.

With a clatter of hooves, they set out.

Once free of the house and garden Joe set his horse to gallop and the chestnut mare took up the pace eagerly.

She felt the wind tug at her veil and skirts. For the first time since yesterday afternoon her heart lightened.

After a good mile or so they drew up at the edge of a sparkling stream and the horses bent their heads to drink.

Joe eyed Henrietta from under the brim of his hat.

"You did not accept the Duke's invitation to tea yesterday," he queried.

"How do you know?" she asked, astonished

"A country house is like an echo chamber. You hear everything in the end."

"Oh," she murmured, reddening as she wondered if Joe had also heard the story of her unhooked dress.

"Well – you see – it turned out that the invitation wasn't for me at all. It was for that other lady the Duke was expecting – Miss Foss."

Joe leaned down to pat his horse's neck.

"Miss Foss, was it? How was that discovered in time?"

"Lady Butterclere told me. D-did the Duke enjoy taking tea with M-Miss Foss?"

"I believe that he was somewhat bemused when she arrived in your place, but he found her uniquely charming."

Henrietta fell silent as Joe glanced sideways at her.

"You did not join the Duke for supper either," he remarked after a moment.

Henrietta was becoming uneasy.

"Are you the D-Duke's official spokesman that you interrogate me so?"

"In a way, yes," he replied. "The Duke would like me to discover why you appear to harbour such apparent distaste for his company."

"*Distaste*? Oh, no," she cried, shocked. "That was not the reason I stayed away at all!"

She could not be sure if Joe heard these last words for something on the far bank had caught his attention and he now reared up in the saddle, staring into the distance.

Henrietta followed his eye.

A man was running across the skyline, right to left, and he was hunched over under the weight of a large sack.

As if he sensed their presence, the man stopped and turned his head their way. Then he was running off again, at greater speed than before, making for some woods.

"Wait here," commanded Joe, digging his heels into Gawain's grey flank as he set out in pursuit.

The man glanced back and ran away faster. Within seconds he had plunged through a wall of briars and was in the woods.

Joe reached the woods, but Gawain baulked at the thorny briar that barred the way.

Faintly over the field, Henrietta heard Joe attempt to urge Gawain on, but to no avail. He finally leaped from the saddle and pushed through the briars without his horse.

A few minutes later Joe emerged carrying the sack, but there was no sign of the man he had been pursuing.

Joe cantered back towards Henrietta.

"Who was that man, Joe, and why did you chase after him?" she asked breathlessly.

"I have no idea *who* he was," said Joe grimly, "but I have a good idea *what* he was. Someone broke into the house late last night. Cook discovered many items missing – a large ham, some chickens, bread, silver cutlery and a sum of money kept in a desk for provisions. Quite a large sum of money, as the ball is imminent."

Here Joe gave the sack a shake.

"The fellow dropped this when he realised it would hinder his escape. I think we'll find most of the items in here – bar the money."

Henrietta stared towards the dark woods, her heart suddenly chilled with fear.

"A p-prisoner escaped yesterday, while we were en route to Merebury," she whispered. "And when we arrived a servant found a hat left behind a trunk. He said we had had a – stowaway."

"No doubt it was our thief."

Joe looked at her pale face and his gaze softened.

"But do not worry. I think we have seen the last of him now."

Henrietta wondered why he was so sure.

"I-I should like to return to the house," she said.

Joe nodded and wheeled his horse around.

The household was fully astir as he and Henrietta clattered back under the arch and into the courtyard.

A stable boy ran out and held the reins while they dismounted.

Henrietta had lifted her skirt and turned towards the house when the boy's voice made her spin round in shock.

"Cook has been asking for you, Your Grace."

Your Grace!

She looked wildly round, but there was no one else the boy could have addressed but Joe.

Joe now swept off his hat and shook his dark locks.

Locks as black as raven's wings.

Her stunned eyes met his.

"Who – who are you?" she whispered.

He unwound the scarf and swept to an elegant bow.

"Joeseph, Duke of Merebury, at your service, Miss Reed."

She thought she would faint.

She stepped back, and back again, and then turned with a cry and took to her heels.

As if she had disturbed his sleep, a black raven rose screeching from the eaves above her and flapped angrily away over the roof.

CHAPTER SIX

"Did you have a good ride out, dear?"

Nanny stood in the doorway of Henrietta's room, her old shawl draped about her and her hair unpinned.

Henrietta leaned down quickly to unhook her boots. She had been crouched broodingly in the armchair for over an hour, weeping tears of frustration, and she did not want Nanny to see her stained cheeks.

"It was – fine, Nanny," she murmured. "Fine."

Nanny looked perplexed. She had been expecting Henrietta to return rosy with health and eyes sparkling with pleasure. Instead of which her charge seemed subdued.

"Who accompanied you on the ride?"

Henrietta started on the other boot.

"The – the Duke's groom – Joe," she replied in as light a tone as she could muster.

Nanny was not deceived. Something was troubling the girl.

"Did anything improper occur?"

Henrietta looked up in alarm. She really must not let Nanny get ideas like *that* into her head.

"Oh, it's not at all what you think, Nanny. It's just that the D–Joe tried to apprehend a thief, who got away though – Joe managed to retrieve the items he had stolen. The whole incident unsettled me rather.

"I am sure the thief is the villain from *The Boston*

Queen, the prisoner who escaped on the road and probably hid on one of the coaches bringing us here to Merebury."

"My goodness!" breathed Nanny. "To think that you were in such danger while I was all tucked up in bed!"

"Oh, I was quite safe. I was in good hands."

Good hands indeed!

That the Duke had courage and command could not be denied, but he had played her just like – like a fish on a hook. Allowed her to believe he was a groom, someone with whom she could feel completely at ease.

She had even ridden *full saddle* in his presence!

This, added to the fact that he had witnessed her in a state of semi-undress the day before, made her redden with shame and indignation.

What must he think of her? Was she a source of entertainment for him?

She had heard of the merry licence of the Prince of Wales and his retinue. Was she now to be the subject of merriment at some future royal supper?

Her head ached as she imagined him recounting his morning's sojourn not just to the Prince, but also to Lady Butterclere and Miss Foss. How they would snigger at the thought of her gullibility. How they would enjoy the idea of her discomfiture.

Why did he do it, *why*?

She now cast her mind back to that first encounter.

Henrietta had to be honest and admit to herself that he had not deliberately misled her until he realised that she took him for the groom.

Then he had announced himself to be simply 'Joe'.

He had clearly mistaken *her* for Romany.

Perhaps initially he had been merely teasing the girl

he thought to be his prospective fiancée, amused that she did not recognise him from the photographs she had seen.

But why did he not reveal himself when he realised his mistake? And why had he then compounded his error by inviting her to ride out with him the following morning?

It could only be that he wanted to arm himself with an amusing episode to recount to his Royal friend!

Henrietta started at a hand on her forehead.

"You're somewhat feverish," frowned Nanny. "We can't have you taking ill, not with the ball this evening."

"Yes, and rehearsals are at midday."

"Well, it's not nine o'clock yet. I tell you what. I'll ring for your breakfast to be brought up here and then you go back to bed for a couple of hours. A little more sleep will do you the world of good."

Henrietta felt a surge of relief at this suggestion.

She felt weary and helpless, and just in the mood to be pampered!

She was about to undress when there was a knock on the door and a pageboy staggered in with an enormous vase of flowers.

"More flowers?" she queried in surprise as there was already a winter bouquet in the room from her arrival.

"All grown in the glasshouse," said the pageboy.

"But – but who has sent them up?" asked Henrietta. "Lady Butterclere?"

"Oh lord, no! It were the Duke what ordered them. Anything more, miss?"

"N-no, thank you," murmured Henrietta.

The page boy withdrew as she stared at the flowers.

They were by way of an apology, she felt at last.

This gesture of the Duke's in no way assuaged her sense of humiliation.

Her silly fantasies about the Duke were truly over.

She had to go through with the performance tonight but after that she hoped she never, never had to set eyes on this house and its illustrious occupant again!

*

Rehearsals did not, at first, go well.

Lady Butterclere insisted on sitting in with Romany and made loud comments throughout every number. She was particularly voluble whenever Henrietta played solo.

"It's a great shame the *real* piano player missed the boat at Boston," she remarked cattily. "Miss Reed is only a pale imitation, I should imagine."

Eddie gestured to Henrietta to stop playing. Laying down his baton, he turned to Lady Butterclere.

"Lady, you are not helping," he muttered wearily. "I would sure appreciate it if you would take yourself and Lizzie there somewhere else."

Lady Butterclere drew herself up her lips quivering.

"You seem to forget, young man, *I* am the reason you are here at all. If I wish to be certain of the quality of your work, I will. And Miss Foss's name is *not* Lizzie."

Eddie regarded her for a moment and then picked up his baton. Turning back to the orchestra, he gave a nod at the brass section. There was a wicked look in his eye.

A moment later the noise became unbearable. Lady Butterclere and Miss Foss pressed their hands to their ears.

"Oh, stop it – do!" cried Lady Butterclere.

"Gotta practice the difficult bits," shouted Eddie.

Grimacing painfully she rose from her seat.

"Come, Romany, we have things to do," said Lady Butterclere loudly. "We must take the carriage into town and buy some attire suitable for this English weather."

87

They hurried away and with a clash of the cymbals, the orchestra ceased playing and fell into laughter.

Even Henrietta, who had been rather withdrawn all morning, gave a wan smile.

Rehearsals proceeded as normal after that, though Henrietta was not happy with her performance. She knew that she was slow and uninspired.

Eddie threw her a shrewd look now and then, but he seemed to have decided not to put any pressure on her.

She felt even more despair later that day when she stood peeping through one of the long gallery windows at the carriages rolling up in the courtyard below.

Below were the guests who had been invited to dine before the ball. One by one the carriages disgorged their occupants and her cheeks grew more and more pale.

She recognised Lord Oxberry, Sir Hugh Waldemar, the Duke and Duchess of Colehill – she had met them all before, either at Lushwood or in the salons of London.

Though these encounters had taken place over four years ago, she knew she had not changed much since then.

At length she hurried along to Kitty's room where Eddie awaited her.

Kitty had found another gown for her to wear. It was an emerald green satin with flounces and an even more plunging neckline than the scarlet dress.

Kitty had also unearthed elbow-length green satin gloves and a tiara studded with green rhinestones.

Henrietta looked dubiously at the gown.

"It's rather like a – a – "

"A saloon girl's dress? Kitty supplied. "Honey, it's just what it is. I got one of the seamstresses here to add the flounces. Just to make it a little more respectable."

'*Respectable,*' thought Henrietta in despair. It was hardly that, although it was undeniably eye-catching.

"I know what you're thinking," said Eddie, "you're thinking that you don't want to be recognised wearing *that*. But worry not. No one will recognise you – for hark!"

He jokingly put a hand to his ear as a knock on the door sounded.

"I do believe the great Lando has arrived."

He then pulled open the door and a small fat man with a powdered face came mincing in, a large black case in his hand. He put the case down and turned to throw an appreciative eye over Henrietta.

"Exquisite!" he pronounced. "It will be such a sad pleasure to hide such natural beauty!"

Henrietta realised that he was the make-up man that Eddie had summoned from London.

"Sit down, my dear," invited Lando.

Henrietta took the seat nervously and stared glumly at her reflection. The next moment Lando had tilted her head and began to apply some scented unguent to her face.

He was hard at his task for a good half an hour.

Henrietta had almost dozed off when Lando at last whisked away the cloth from her shoulders.

"Finis!" he cried.

Henrietta opened her eyes and gave a gasp of shock at the sight that confronted her.

Her eyes were heavily lined with kohl, giving her a sleepy gaze. Her ivory skin was concealed beneath a beige paste of some sort and her cheeks were almost purple with rouge. Her lips were scarlet, heavily outlined in black.

Before she even had time to digest her look, Lando held something sleek and black over her head and the next minute he was fitting it down over her helpless skull.

It was a wig.

"You look every inch the professional showgirl," proclaimed Eddie.

"B-but I don't want to look like a showgirl!"

"Harrie, I know," Eddie soothed her. "But this way, nobody, but *nobody* is going to recognise you, are they?"

Henrietta looked at herself again. Eddie was right, she scarcely recognised herself. Every trace of Henrietta Radford – let alone Harrietta Reed – had been eliminated. She looked older and wiser and – much, much harder.

The dress will certainly suit me now, she thought.

She had no doubt that the Duke of Merebury would enjoy pointing her garishly garbed figure out to the Prince of Wales!

The musicians had supper in the servants hall.

Then they hurried to the ballroom where they were in place and striking up as the doors were thrown open for the Prince of Wales and his retinue.

The Royal stare swept appreciatively all round the room and over the orchestra.

Eddie gave a cheeky deep bow which the Prince of Wales graciously acknowledged.

The other guests surged in behind the Prince.

Henrietta tried not to look but her eyes, lashes laden with mascara, continually flicked at the those milling about on the floor.

She could see Mrs. Poody beaming on the arm of an elderly Admiral and could not but smile to herself.

Then she caught sight of the Duke.

The dishevelled tousled Joe had disappeared. In his place was a tall commanding figure in black evening dress and white gloves.

His hair was all smoothed back, revealing a dark, brooding brow and hooded eyes. He was by far the most handsome man in the room.

Henrietta tore her gaze away from him to examine his companions, Romany and Lady Butterclere.

Romany was in a most unbecoming pink. Her hair, piled unsteadily high, threatened to topple at each nod of her head. Her hand lay like a claw on the Duke's forearm.

Lady Butterclere was in an innocuous blue muslin, the mild colour belying the baleful glare of her eye.

Henrietta stole another glance at the Duke.

To her horror she saw he was now looking directly her way, his forehead furrowing as he took in her outfit.

She looked quickly down at the keyboard, a blush suffusing her face, surging up her cheeks beneath the rouge and making it seem even more vivid.

For the rest of the evening she never once looked up from the piano.

She relinquished herself up to the music, accepting with gratitude its power to soothe.

At last she began to forget her surroundings, forget the Duke, Romany and Lady Butterclere. Eyes closed, her body swaying, she seemed increasingly consumed by some deep and secret passion and her playing became inspired.

The interval came and Henrietta's hands dropped to her lap, but it was a moment or two before she was fully aware of the tumultuous applause.

"Bravo! Bravo!" cried the Prince of Wales.

The orchestra was clearly a huge success.

Champagne was brought to the dais for the players.

Still in a daze, Henrietta accepted a glass. She took a sip and almost sneezed as the bubbles danced in her nose.

"Harrie?" Eddie was hovering by her with a smile. "The Prince of Wales would like to be introduced to you."

"T-to me?" echoed Henrietta fearfully.

"Yes," nodded Eddie. "He wants to meet us all, but he particularly asked for *you*."

"Eddie, I c-can't."

All confidence in her disguise had gone. Surely the Prince would recognise her under all the powder and paint?

Eddie held out his hand.

"I don't know much about your English customs, but even *I* understand that no one refuses a Prince."

Henrietta blinked unhappily and then rose, taking Eddie's arm and allowing herself to be led from the dais.

"Quite a performer!" came a hearty voice.

Henrietta glanced up at the Prince of Wales's genial features and gave a small curtsy.

"Your – Royal Highness," was all she could reply, her gaze roving to where the Duke was standing.

The Prince was surveying her with interest, but not recognition.

"The effect upon the eye of your costume is so very American," he commented.

"Our exact intention, Your Royal Highness!" Eddie offered quickly.

Henrietta curtsied again, aware now that the Duke kept turning to throw a still puzzled glance her way.

"You must be delighted to have discovered such a unique talent, Mr. Bragg," the Prince was musing.

"I am," said Eddie, before adding with a theatrical sigh, "I fear, however, that I may lose her before long – "

"Not, I hope, before you agree to come and play for *me*?" demanded the Prince.

Eddie hesitated, throwing at Henrietta a meaningful look, which she studiously avoided.

She was *not* going to commit herself to playing for the Prince of Wales just to accommodate *his* ambitions!

Eddie understood her silence.

"I may not be able to persuade her to stay – "

"Pity, pity," muttered the Prince. "Well, we'll see, we'll see."

He turned to his *aide-de-camp* and instructed him to take Eddie's card.

Henrietta imagined that she was now free to return to what she considered was the safety of the dais.

She was uncomfortable at being on the floor, where anyone present might scrutinise her at close quarters.

As she gathered up her skirts and turned, however, she was arrested by the voice of the Duke.

"Do you need your pianist for the next number?" she heard him ask Eddie.

She could see Eddie give a nonchalant shrug.

"I reckon I can do without Miss Reed for a melody or two," he responded with a knowing smile.

The Duke turned to Henrietta.

"Then, madam, I trust that you will agree to offer me the next dance?"

Henrietta was confused beyond measure.

What sort of game was the Duke playing now?

It was one thing for the Prince to address himself to the members of the orchestra. Surely it was quite another for the host to lead the piano player – particularly one who resembled nothing so much as a tawdry showgirl – out on to the floor?

She cast frantic glances about her. For once she

hoped for the intervention of Lady Butterclere, who would surely not countenance the Duke in this request. But she and Romany Foss were trailing in the wake of the Prince's retinue, eager for the least crumb of Royal attention.

Eddie leaped back onto the dais and lifted his baton as Henrietta gazed ruefully after him.

"Madam?"

The Duke stepped forward and held out his hand to her. Hesitatingly, she turned and head low placed her hand in his.

It was just as if a jolt of electricity passed between them. She almost gasped out aloud at the sensation that thrilled through her limbs.

At the very same time he gave a barely perceptible shudder, closing his fingers over hers so tightly that her hand was caught as in a vice.

She gave a low soft moan and the Duke, checking himself, loosened his grip.

"Do I still hurt you, madam?" he asked in a low voice.

"N-not now, Your Grace."

He was then silent for so long that at last she raised her eyes to his. His black pupils were dilated, shining with almost unbearable intensity as he feasted on her features.

"God, madam, but even under that ridiculous paint, you draw the eye," he muttered.

Henrietta began to tremble and her skin seemed to burn under his gaze, a gaze that now lingered on her lips.

If he did not look away soon, she would certainly faint. Faint with the longing to raise herself on tiptoe and meet his mouth with hers –

She was unutterably relieved as the orchestra struck up and the Duke drew her in one swift move to his breast.

There she could at least hide her scalded face for a moment and recover her disturbed senses.

She might not have moved at all, but the Duke's arms, strong and insistent, urged her into a slow waltz.

Raising her head as she circled round the floor, she glimpsed Mrs. Poody's startled stare.

Then Lady Butterclere's mouth open in outrage and astonishment. Next, Romany, her hairdo bobbing on her head with indignation.

This was very cruel of the Duke, thought Henrietta, *cruel*! Yet the beat of his heart so close to hers did not feel cruel. His breath, stirring the curls on her forehead, did not feel cruel. His fingers entwining hers did not feel cruel.

'*What is happening to me*?' she cried to herself in alarm.

She tried to twist away from the Duke's breast, but his arm around her waist tightened and he bent his head to her ear.

"What, do you still harbour such distaste for the company of the Duke of Merebury?" he murmured.

Henrietta flushed.

"The last time I was asked a question like that," she replied stiffly, "it was posed by a certain Joe the g-groom."

"The last time I heard an answer to a question like that," replied the Duke gravely, "it was given by a certain Miss Harrietta Reed – not by *Sadie the saloon girl*."

Henrietta flushed an even deeper red.

"M-meaning?"

The Duke raised his eyebrow.

"Meaning we both seem to have a certain talent for disguise!"

Henrietta was flustered.

What on earth would he say if he knew that she was actually in disguise *twice over*, that the person he knew as Miss Reed was as unauthentic as – *Sadie the saloon girl*?

"I ask again," he persisted. "Do you still harbour a distaste for my company?"

Henrietta closed her eyes. Oh, how she wished she could confess that her heart was now opening like a flower beneath his blazing scrutiny, her flesh melting like snow at his urgent touch.

Yet she dared not – could not!

He was destined for another and she had become known to him in such a way that all future contact between them was impossible.

She must remain Harrietta Reed to him or forfeit forever any shred of respect he might have for her.

"I h-have no feelings regarding your presence one way or the other," she ventured lamely. "It's just that I-I do not feel I should be – dancing with you like this since I am nothing but a – a mere piano player."

"Never '*mere*'," added the Duke softly. "You are – exceptional. I could not take my eyes from you when you were playing. You seemed to deliver yourself up, to burn with devotion and I could not help but wonder what other cause might elicit such devouring passion – "

His words trailed away.

When she looked up, his jaw had tightened as if he was forcing himself to say no more.

She cast about for some innocuous response to his words, but could find none.

The two whirled on in silence, his brow indicating a struggle within himself that she, lost in new sensations, did not notice.

The ardour in his voice stirred her and rendered her helpless in his arms.

She felt herself lost as never before to the moment.

'Everything would be just perfection,' she sighed to herself, 'if only I was here as Miss Radford and not Miss Reed and if only Romany Foss *did not exist*!'

The Duke's voice now intruded on what she guiltily knew to be an uncharitable thought.

"So, Miss Reed, what other unlikely talents do you possess? Apart from playing the piano?"

The unexpected levity of his tone confused her.

"Oh, I can hunt racoon and shoot rapids and play poker – as well as any man!" she responded airily.

The Duke threw back his head with a laugh.

"*Touché*, Miss Reed," he murmured.

The music ended with a flourish.

Henrietta imagined the Duke would release her and she began to withdraw her hand from his. To her surprise, however, his grip tightened yet again.

"I am not yet ready to let you go, madam," he said.

Exclaiming, she found herself swiftly manoeuvred through the open French doors and out onto the terrace.

She was glad of the fresh breeze on her hot cheeks.

They stood, she panting, he taking deep controlling breaths, his eyes fixed on her face.

"So what is this all about?" he demanded.

"W-what do you mean?"

"*This*! The dress – the make-up – the wig?"

She wondered at his concern. What did it matter to him how she chose to appear at a performance?

"It – it's how Eddie wants me to l-look."

The Duke's eyes narrowed.

"Or how *you* wish to look?"

Stung at his derision, she drew herself up.

"I have answered your question, Your Grace, which is more than I am required to do, I am not your s-servant."

She did not read his expression as he stared at her. His eyes were dark, the lids lowered over inky depths.

"Indeed you are not," he answered at last. "Forgive me. I accept your rebuke."

Yet he did not tear his gaze away from her face for a second – it travelled down her face, from her hair to her large liquid eyes to her red bow-shaped lips.

He lingered at length on her lips, his head inclining as if wishing to meet them with his own –

Beyond him, in the shadows, Henrietta espied the tiny red glow of a cigar.

"There is s-somebody – here," she muttered.

The Duke straightened and slowly turned. Too late! The red glow was extinguished.

"There *was* somebody there, I am sure – just by that open window," Henrietta insisted.

The Duke said nothing.

"I-I should g-go, Your Grace," mumbled Henrietta uneasily. "Eddie will be wanting me to resume playing."

"You are not dismissed!" he retorted.

"I – beg your pardon?"

Henrietta was shocked.

"I have said before, I am not your s-servant. You have no right to – give me such orders."

The Duke turned on her savagely.

"Damn you, but I *do* have a right! Tonight, at least,

I have the right, for tonight I am paying your wages! And I wish you to remain here until I understand what it is about you that so – disturbs and incites a man! Quite against his better instincts!"

His better instincts!

Henrietta's lips trembled.

The Duke was reminding her that Miss Reed and by default Sadie the saloon girl were not the kind of women who would normally come within his sphere of interest.

The chasm between their world and his was clearly insurmountable.

Yet it was unfair of him to address her in this way.

"T-then will you p-please now employ your better instincts and l-let me go indoors," she asked haltingly.

For an answer, he then took Henrietta's chin in his hand and held her face up to his. Tugging a handkerchief from his pocket, he roughly applied it to her lips.

Though she twisted her head back and forth, it was only a moment before all traces of her scarlet lipstick were removed.

"Now, madam," he breathed softly, "there are your own ruby lips exposed. And no instinct exists within me beyond the desire to claim your pretty mouth for mine – "

A sudden and unwelcome voice arrested him.

"Your Grace? Your Grace? Are you out there?"

A curse escaped his lips. He relinquished his hold on Henrietta and moved from her side as Lady Butterclere and Romany careered through the French windows.

"I have been looking for you all over," complained Lady Butterclere, as she caught sight of Henrietta and gave a furious snort. "What! *You* are out here too?"

Henrietta still trembling from the Duke's words and touch, now dropped her gaze.

"They were dancing," piped up Romany, gnawing viciously at one of her fingernails.

"Yes most inappropriate," sniffed Lady Butterclere. "Romany, dear, take your fingers out of your mouth. And you, Miss Reed – *desist*."

"I-I'm sorry?" Henrietta looked up, bewildered.

"Desist, I say. You are a common conniver and my stepbrother should beware. Your conduct could very soon be the talk of – "

The Duke raised a warning hand.

"Madam, you forget where you are," he said icily.

"I certainly do not forget *where* I am or *who* I am," responded Lady Butterclere heatedly. "I am the stepsister of the Duke of Merebury and it is my duty to protect his good name and standing wherever I see it threatened. Miss Reed here has already compromised her reputation."

As the Duke drew in his breath, Henrietta rounded on Lady Butterclere in outraged disbelief.

"What on earth do you mean?" she demanded.

"On *The Boston Queen*," replied Lady Butterclere grandly, "did you or did you not enter the Second Class section of the ship on more than one occasion?"

"Yes, I did, but – "

"And was that not for the sole purpose of meeting Mr. Eddie Bragg?"

"I met him there, yes, but that was not the sole – "

Lady Butterclere turned in triumph to the Duke.

"There you are – stepbrother. She is Eddie Bragg's creature. Her attire tonight tells you everything. Need I elaborate more?"

Henrietta turned imploring eyes upon the Duke, but he would not look her way. He stood, his jaw flexing, his eyes black as the night sky.

Then he turned on his heels and strode to the house.

"Stepsister – Miss Foss – let us go in," he snapped over his shoulder.

Henrietta was stunned and barely able to breathe.

She had made no play for the Duke.

It was he who had pressed *her* to dance, he who had led her out here onto the terrace. Whatever struggle had ensued in his breast had not been of her doing.

Oh, how she wished that she had never come here to Merebury Court. It might have been that some time in the future Henrietta Radford would meet the Duke at some London party and be introduced on equal terms.

Even had he then been married to Romany Foss, he would at least not have regarded her with such contempt. He would not have talked to her against his better instincts.

Henrietta now pressed her hands to her face with a groan. Tears welled through her fingers.

She did not hear footsteps cross the terrace until it was too late.

"We are meeting again, Miss Radford."

She froze in utter disbelief. That voice. It was not possible. Not *here*. Surely she was hearing things?

Slowly she took her hands from her face.

When she saw who was standing sneeringly before her, she gave a strangled cry and fell in a dead faint on the stones.

Prince Vasily of Rumania stood quietly stroking his moustache before he then leaned down and scooped up the unconscious Henrietta into his arms.

CHAPTER SEVEN

"She is stirring."

"Step back there, give her some air."

"Water, somebody."

Henrietta felt the rim of a glass thrust onto her lips, then water. She drank a few sips and opened her eyes.

She was lying on a couch in what seemed to be the library. Anxious faces peered down at her.

Neither the Duke nor Romany nor Lady Butterclere was there, but she recognised Eddie, Kitty and Nanny.

She glimpsed the Prince of Wales as well, watching with concern from the doorway.

Of Prince Vasily there was no sign at all.

Nanny clapped her hands in such relief as Henrietta struggled to sit upright.

"Thank Heavens," crowed the old lady.

Eddie hurried to put a cushion at Henrietta's back.

"What happened, Harrie?" he asked.

"I was out on the terrace and I must have fainted."

"The first we knew of it was when that gentleman carried you in," commented Kitty.

"T-that gentleman. W-where is he now?"

Kitty glanced about and shrugged.

"Not here. He deposited you on the couch and then faded into the background. I think he needed a drink!"

Henrietta beckoned to Nanny and she leaned close.

"D-did you recognise him?"

"No, to be honest, dear, I was too concerned about you. Why, who was it?

"Prince V-Vasily," Henrietta told her quietly.

Nanny's hand flew to her mouth.

"But he wasn't in his costume at all. He was got up like an English gentleman. In evening dress with a cape."

"Yes. I know."

Henrietta sank back and closed her eyes.

Her heart was trembling in her breast. What was Prince Vasily doing in England? What was he doing at the ball? Had he been invited or had he come seeking herself?

"Harrie?" It was Eddie kneeling by the couch.

"Yes, Eddie?"

"I've got to get the orchestra going again. Do you feel up to playing?"

"Could I have just a little while – to myself?"

"Sure. We'll play a few more waltzes. Those don't need the piano. You join us when you're ready."

The Prince of Wales called from the doorway.

"How is the young lady?"

"She's okay, Your Royal Highness. What she'd like is for us all to leave her so she can compose herself."

With sympathetic murmurs all the guests who had flooded into the library now moved away.

Nanny was the last, hovering at the door.

"You're sure, you're all right?" she fussed.

Henrietta nodded and Nanny closed the library door behind her.

The silence was most welcome. There was just the

faint crackle of logs in the hearth and then, from the distant ballroom, the violins struck up.

How amazed the guests must have been as Prince Vasily burst through the terrace door, Henrietta in his arms.

The Duke, Lady Butterclere and Romany must not have been present. No doubt they were ensconced in his study discussing the character of Miss Harrietta Reed!

Henrietta twisted her hands together unhappily.

How meanly the Duke had treated her and his poor fiancée.

He had meant to kiss her, she was sure of that.

She was equally sure that she would have let him.

She could not forget the magic of his touch nor the flare of passion in his dark eyes. The dance had unleashed in her a scalding desire to be in his arms.

She thought of Prince Vasily. Her skin crawled as she envisaged his hands on her body – her breast crushed against his.

Where was the ghastly creature now, she wondered.

This was no good!

She must compose herself, as Eddie had said. She had to go to the piano and play as if nothing had happened.

She took another sip of water and swung her feet to the floor. She rose feeling unsteady. She would just take a few steps round the library till she felt fully herself.

Firelight flickered on endless leather bound books.

Henrietta trailed her fingers along the spines as she circled the room. She always loved reading and she paused at a section devoted to works in Latin.

Here was Julius Caesar's *Gallic Wars*.

She took the book from the shelf and opened it.

"So as well as hunting and shooting and poker, you read Latin as well?"

Henrietta almost dropped the tome from her hands.

The Duke stood surveying her from the doorway.

"I – yes, I do –Your Grace."

"I suppose you read French too and even German?"

"B-both," Henrietta confessed reluctantly.

She turned and slipped the book back into the shelf, her intention being to leave the library as soon as possible.

The Duke, however, had other ideas. He stepped in to the room and closed the double doors behind him.

He advanced on Henrietta, who could feel herself shrinking against the bookshelves.

"You are a most intriguing creation," he murmured, as he halted not three feet from her.

"C-creation?"

"Why yes." His eyes ran appraisingly up and down her body. "A young lady who rides akimbo and yet reads Latin. A painted showgirl who can play the piano like a professional at the Conservatoire. Just who are you, Miss Reed, and from whom do you hide?"

"H-hide?"

"Are you a parrot, that you echo me so?"

"P-parrot?"

"Oh, for God's sake, answer me!" he exploded.

Henrietta felt her head swim with alarm.

The Duke was suspicious.

Suppose he forced the truth from her lips – that her blood was as blue as his, that she was disgracing her class and her good family name.

The damage this might do to her father's reputation made her feel sick with remorse.

She began to sway, her hands groping the shelves behind her for support. Colour drained from her cheeks and she felt herself slide slowly down –

The Duke was all attention. He sprang forward and caught her, lifting her in his arms and carrying her back to the couch.

"You did not rest long for enough," he scolded her solicitously. "Should I call for Mrs. Poody?"

Henrietta shook her head as his hand wavered.

"Why is it I – cannot keep away?" he whispered, so low it was almost to himself. "Why is it I cannot heed my stepsister's warnings?"

He traced a finger across her eyelids and down her cheek and it seemed as if he scored a trail across her flesh, so exquisite was the combination of pleasure and pain.

Pleasure that it was his hand and pain that it was his hand too. For it must not be, it could not be, should not be. This hand should caress Romany – not Harrietta Reed.

Yet pleasure won.

His hand so close by was too much of a temptation. She caught it in her own and brought it lovingly to her lips.

The Duke's nostrils flared above her.

His eyes flashed. He twisted his hand so that hers was trapped, clenching hard so that her fingers felt crushed.

His voice was choked, husky and urgent.

"Madam, I must ask you – are you free to do that?"

Henrietta's eyes widened.

"Am *I* free?" she gasped.

How dare he broach the subject, when his fiancée was only yards away, dancing in blissful ignorance?

The Duke seemed unrepentant of his question.

"Oh, God, God," he groaned. "If only I knew who

or what you are and to whom, if *anyone*, you belonged!"

Henrietta tugged her hand free of his and stumbled to her feet. She must end all this now. She must not give in to her longing or further compromise her position.

"Where are you going?"

She was already at the door.

"Your Grace, I – must rejoin the orchestra."

"Ah. Eddie Bragg is awaiting!" said the Duke with a degree of bitterness.

"My *companions* are waiting for me," she replied firmly.

With that, she opened the door and fled.

*

"You played as well as Paderewski!" pronounced the Prince of Wales enthusiastically.

"T-thank you, sir, t-thank you," muttered Henrietta, barely conscious of the Prince's words.

She did not know, in truth, how she had managed to perform. Her fingers seemed to move of their own accord while her frantic eyes scanned the throng of dancers.

She was aware that the Duke had entered and was dancing with Romany, but for the moment at least, though her heart ached, the Duke was not her focus.

No, it was Prince Vasily she was trying to track.

On more than one occasion she had looked up from the piano to see him watching her with a curl of his lip.

And then she glimpsed him circling the floor with a partner – Lady Butterclere. This sight had set her pulse racing in horror.

What might he divulge?

"Ah, and here is our host to add his congratulations to mine," the Prince of Wales was saying.

Henrietta stiffened as the Duke approached.

"I was just saying that Miss Reed here displays a touch of genius at the piano," enthused the Prince.

The Duke did not look at Henrietta.

"She has displayed a touch of genius throughout the evening," he concurred icily.

Henrietta reddened.

"Well," added the Prince of Wales, "I must have a word with the rest of the orchestra. They were all superb."

"I will accompany you, sir," suggested the Duke.

As they turned away, her heart pounded. She must find out how or why Prince Vasily was attending the ball. She must tell the Duke about him, although God knew she wished herself a hundred miles or so away from his all too powerful presence.

"Y-your Grace?"

"Yes?"

He stopped and turned, his eyes cool.

"T-that man, dancing with your – stepsister – "

"Yes," he said impatiently. "It was he who carried you in from the terrace. His name is Prince Vasily and it was Miss Foss who requested he be invited. What is it you wish to know about him?"

"N-nothing – "

Henrietta shrank into herself in horror.

Romany Foss had invited Prince Vasily! How on earth was Miss Foss acquainted with him?

The Duke, somewhat despite himself, was intrigued by the way she seemed so concerned about Prince Vasily.

"Were you by any chance already acquainted with Prince Vasily before tonight?" he enquired slowly.

The way her stricken eyes flew answered him.

"What other secrets do you harbour in your breast, Miss Reed?" he remarked grimly.

Henrietta, dismayed beyond any measure, could do nothing else but turn and rush from his side.

She stumbled into the hall and sank into a chair and closed her eyes, having no strength to mount the stairs.

The idea of being Miss Reed had at first struck her as an adventure, playing with the orchestra a jest. A stay at Merebury seemed fortuitous, a fun way of exploring where her fascination with its owner, the Duke, had originated.

Now it was turning into a nightmare. She had been a fool – an immature and untried fool.

She buried her face in her hands – how she longed to be safely home at Lushwood!

"You are suffering, I hope, Miss Radford?"

Henrietta's eyes flew open.

"You!" she gasped.

"I – yes," leered Prince Vasily.

"W-what do you want?"

"Only to tell you, not to worry. If this Duke does not want you – and I will make certain he does *not* want you – then *I* do."

She swallowed, looking desperately around the hall for a friendly face.

"You are mad," she whispered. "*Mad!*"

Prince Vasily regarded her idly, his fingers running along his thin moustache.

How had she ever found him in any way attractive?

"W-what are you doing here?" she asked him.

"Ah, my history since you sent me away? I will tell you. I discover you are leaving, so I sail with you –"

"You were on *The Boston Queen*? And you were the man who – was arrested on board?"

He shrugged, spreading his hands wide in a gesture of helplessness.

"A small disagreement with a card player. Such a fuss. In my country, these matters are settled without the law." He loomed in menacingly over Henrietta. "Just as affairs of honour are settled without the law!"

She stared at him. Spittle hung on his swollen lip.

"But you escaped the law. How did you get here?"

"To Merebury?" he smirked. "Hidden right behind a trunk, my sweet, like a common coach boy."

'So he was the stowaway too,' she mused, 'and, no doubt, the thief the Duke had pursued.'

She gazed fearfully up at him.

"Y-you have been following me?"

"Oh, yes, little lark. If I desire a woman, does she ever escape me? *Never*!"

"But tonight – how is it that you are dressed like that – and at the ball?"

Prince Vasily licked the spittle from his lips.

"How? I tell you. I acquire a little money."

"By stealing from this very house," she muttered.

Prince Vasily seemed not to hear.

"I go to town to take lodgings," he continued, "and then I go to buy clothes. I recognise Miss Foss and Lady Butterclere. I have seen them in the coach coming here, when I am a secret passenger.

"When Miss Foss is alone I introduce myself to her. I am a lonely Prince, travelling Europe. How I would love to visit one of the great English houses. I make the eyes at her and she is flattered. She invites me to the ball."

He spread his hands in a wide gesture.

"Do I not have the ingenious mind?"

"Not so ingenious, Prince. For you have revealed yourself to me and I will make it known that you are a thief and – and an imposter."

Prince Vasily showed his teeth.

"An imposter? Like you, Miss *Radford*?"

Henrietta had half risen, but now she sank back.

Of course! She should have realised at once.

If she exposed *him,* he would expose *her.*

He watched her, his face creased with satisfaction.

"Did I not warn you, so many days ago, in Boston," he sneered. *"You will regret such treatment of me!"*

"You – are a m-monster," moaned Henrietta.

Prince Vasily leaned closer, until his face was only inches from hers.

"Tell me, have you ever been kissed by a monster, Miss Radford?" he whispered.

Before she could reply, his mouth was on hers, his tongue forcing itself through her lips.

She broke away panting, only to see, watching with malicious glee from the foot of the stairs, Lady Butterclere.

"I was about to retire," smirked Lady Butterclere. "But how can I, when such interesting things are going on – in the hallway, of all places!"

Prince Vasily wiped his moustache and gave a bow.

"Lady Butterclere," he waved his hand at Henrietta. "I am just renewing my acquaintance with this lady."

"*Are* you? Your attentions seemed most welcome, I must say."

Henrietta scrambled to her feet, her breast heaving.

"His intentions are not welcome, Lady Butterclere, and never will be!" she cried.

Lady Butterclere regarded her icily.

"Your reputation, if you do have one to speak of," she sneered, "is rapidly becoming mud! *Mud*!"

She turned and proceeded haughtily up the stairs.

Prince Vasily's amused eyes danced over Henrietta.

"There is only one way to restore your reputation, my lark," he said. "And that is to marry me. Which, for a consideration from your Papa, I would agree to do."

Henrietta shrank from his gaze – his lascivious and unwelcome gaze.

"Never!" she wailed. "*Never*!"

His laughter echoed in her ears as she ran down the nearest corridor, careering into a bemused footman.

She did not know where she wanted to go, except to put as a great a distance as possible between herself and the revolting Prince Vasily.

Her flight was feverish and unthinking. She tugged the wig off and threw it to one side, as if she might thus discard the whole sorry evening and leave it all behind her.

On she ran, passing kitchens and pantries, on and on, until she hurtled through a large oak door and almost fell into the sweetest of night air.

She was in the same courtyard where she had first met the Duke – or Joe the groom, as she had believed then.

She paused, blood thumping in her temples. Then she went on, out under the arch and into the gardens at the back of the great house.

She stopped running and gazed about. To her right was the entrance to what looked like a maze. To her left, steps led down to a lake, gleaming under the moonlight.

Henrietta began to descend the first flight of steps.

She felt calmer now and decided to walk to the lake and back. Then she would go back to her bed.

First thing tomorrow morning she and Nanny must leave and with luck they might shake off Prince Vasily.

She was about to descend the second flight of steps when a voice from the darkness called out to her.

"Who's there?"

She spun round and from a bench in the shadow of a wall the figure of a man rose and came forward.

It was the Duke.

For a second they both stood as if turned to stone. Neither could tear their eyes from the other.

The Duke's face in the moonlight was a marvel of granite, chiselled to perfection. His mouth was set, his lips stern. His eyes were black as pitch, black and unyielding as the night. Yet there was heat in his gaze.

Henrietta had a wild look about her. Her hair had fallen loose of the pins that had secured it under the wig. It now lay dishevelled over her shoulders, stirring in the night breeze.

Her eyes were huge, as if full of moonlight. The black flounce about her neckline had come away.

"Madam, it seems as if you are in distress," he said at last in a low voice.

"I? N-no. I am – just enjoying the night air."

The Duke opened his mouth as if to say more, but a complaining voice sounded behind him.

"Who has now interrupted us, Joseph? We were just settling down so cosy together."

Henrietta blinked in dismay as Romany Foss rose from the bench.

"Oh, it's you," sniffed Romany. "What are you after out here, I wonder?"

Henrietta stepped back a pace, her mind in a whirl.

Romany had said '*Joseph.*' She had used the word '*cosy.*' '*Cosy together*!' It was right, she was the Duke's fiancée, and she could speak this way and yet the words struck like the fangs of a snake at Henrietta's heart.

"I am – sorry to have intruded – " she stammered. "I-I will go back."

"Wait, madam!"

The Duke put out his hand.

But Henrietta had fled.

She meant to retrace her steps. She meant to seek the solitude of her room, the comfort of her canopied bed, where secret tears could be shed into her pillow.

Papa, she thought with a sob, as she stumbled up the stone steps. What would he think of her if he could see her now?

The Duke. He had been courting Romany, there on the bench in the shadow of the wall. Courting her in the pale light of the moon. No doubt their engagement would be publicly announced at any moment.

She groaned as she thought of Romany entwined in the Duke's arms.

I am jealous, she admitted to herself. *Jealous*!

She stood recovering her breath for a moment and then looked round.

She was in some kind of alley, narrow, with high hedges on either side. It curved to the right ahead of her and when she looked back, it curved to the left.

She had not noticed the various twists and turns of whichever path she had followed. Now she did not know whether to go forward or back.

After some deliberation, she went forward.

The path veered right and there was a fork. She had the choice of two alleyways and she chose the left one. That too twisted and turned, bringing her to another fork.

Taking the right this time, within minutes she found herself at a dead end.

Then it dawned on her that she was in the maze!

Now her heart began to beat with trepidation.

She had no idea how extensive the maze was and no memory of how she had first entered it.

She must now start by retracing her steps and this she did, or thought she did, but all the alleys looked alike. For all she knew she was going round in circles.

She must leave some marker to indicate which way she had passed, like Theseus in the Minotaur's labyrinth.

Then an idea came to her.

The black flounce!

It was already loose and was flimsy enough for her to be able to tear it into pieces.

She ripped hard at the flounce. As it tore away, the neckline of her dress came with it, exposing the upper part of her breast. Her alabaster skin gleamed in the moonlight.

Shivering, she ripped a piece off and attached it to a bush. Then she walked on, thereby preventing herself from traversing the same alley twice.

But her ingenuity did not help her find the way out. After a quarter of an hour she was exhausted and beginning to despair.

The night air felt no longer sweet, rather it was chill and unpleasantly moist.

Soon all she wished for was somewhere to rest.

As if in answer to her prayers she staggered at last

into a clearing in which stood a stone seat. With a cry she sank upon it, barely noticing how cold it was to the touch.

She looked around then and her heart sank.

There was no doubt but that she was at the centre of the maze. She would never find her way out tonight.

The torrid sense of nightmare that had slowly been enveloping her all evening now fell fully upon her like a heavy shroud.

Under its weight, her limbs turned to ice, her teeth chattered and she lost all control. Her wail of misery was loud and the sobs that followed rent the night air like nails.

How long she wept she did not know.

Only when her breath seemed to freeze in her throat did her cries subside. Now she lay, cold as the tomb, her tears hanging on her cheeks like ice.

She was dimly aware of a soft cape falling around her shoulders and strong arms lifting her.

Shivering and almost unconscious, she felt herself held against a warm breast. Her own breast, half exposed, the skin icy and white as snow, rose and fell heavily.

A tender hand wrapped the cape more tightly about her and then brushed the hair from her forehead.

"What has driven you to run so wildly through the night?" came gentle and concerned tones.

She was too tired to think. She could barely grasp whose voice it was until at last a name came to her.

"Joe!" she murmured, as she felt firm hands reach beneath her body and lift her carefully up.

"Joe!" she sighed as her head fell drowsily against a firm strong shoulder.

And "*Joe,*" she breathed again, as her eyes closed and she fell into a deep and peaceful sleep.

CHAPTER EIGHT

Henrietta woke to find herself in her own bedroom at Merebury, gazing up at the canopy over her bed.

Raising herself unsteadily onto her elbow, she saw that the fire in the wide hearth had been banked high and was sending out a rosy comforting glow.

Nanny dozed in a high chair in her old shawl.

At the window a tall figure leaned, gazing out at the dark sky.

The Duke!

Henrietta's breath caught in her throat and she sank back onto the pillow.

'What is he doing here?' she asked herself wildly.

Indeed, what was *she* doing here?

She had no memory of climbing up the stairs. The last thing she remembered that she had been in the gardens. She had heard a voice say *who's there?* and then –

She almost cried out as the ensuing events flooded back into her mind.

Romany, the maze, the cold, the fear. Then those strong arms lifting her from the chilly stone bench!

The Duke had brought her here to her bed.

Her cheeks flushed as she realised that she was no longer in the green dress she had worn to perform with the orchestra, but in her own white night shift.

The Duke must have called on Nanny to come and

disrobe her. What could Nanny have thought to see her so dishevelled, her hair loose, her breast half exposed?

She peeped at the Duke and now saw that he had something clutched in his hand.

To her astonishment she recognised her dress, its green skirt trailing on the ground,

She closed her eyes.

Seeing the Duke's lithe figure outlined against the window, she could not help but recall the comfort of being held against his strong chest. She had been delirious and was unconscious in his arms yet she was sure that she had heard his heart beating and sure she had felt his kiss brush her damp hair.

Stretching with pleasure at her reminiscences, she opened her eyes.

The Duke was now standing at the foot of the bed, watching her.

Meeting her startled gaze, he put a finger to his lips and moved quietly to her side.

"You have slept well?" he whispered.

"I-I think I have. B-but what time is it?"

He held up a hand in reply, indicating that she must listen and she heard the first faint chime of a distant clock.

One, two, three –

As each note struck, the Duke's gaze intensified.

His eyes seemed to burn through her shift to the very flesh beneath. She felt pinned under his scrutiny like a butterfly. She could not avert her gaze or close her eyes against the blaze of his passionate interest.

The chimes faded away.

"Three o'clock," mumbled Henrietta wonderingly. "I have been asleep some four hours or so?"

"You have indeed."

"H-have you been here all along?"

The Duke gave a faint smile.

"Most of the time. When I carried you in here from the maze I called for Mrs. Poody. You seemed peaceful, but we were both reluctant to leave you alone. Mrs. Poody took up her watch by the fire, giving me leave to come and go through the night.

"If your breathing changed, it was agreed I should send for the doctor. We thought our mutual watch the best procedure as neither of us wished to alarm the household.

"I left you alone for a while as I had other business to attend to."

Henrietta wondered miserably if he meant, by that, Romany Foss.

"But then," went on the Duke, "I returned and have been here ever since."

"I m-must thank you – for your d-dutiful attention," stammered Henrietta.

His gaze swept once again over her prone figure.

"It was rather more than duty that held me here," he confessed.

His gaze fell and lingered on her hand where it lay idly on the satin quilt.

His features were suddenly consumed with such a look of ardent hunger that, even to her, his next question came as no surprise.

"May I take – your hand?" he asked eagerly.

Henrietta threw a fearful look towards Nanny in her chair, but the old lady did not stir.

"If – you so w-wish, Your Grace," she murmured.

The Duke gave a rueful smile.

"A little while ago you called me Joe," he reminded her. He lifted her hand and was turning it over and over in his as if marvelling at its composition.

"It is so pale – so translucent – the veins so near the surface," he said softly.

Sighing he brought it to his lips – lips that trembled as they pressed against her palm.

Henrietta drew in her breath.

What did the Duke mean by such an intimate act as this? He was not like all the others who had courted her.

He could have no interest in her fortune, for he had no idea she possessed one. Furthermore, he was already wealthy in his own right.

It was reckless of the Duke – they were not alone in the room – he had a fiancée – it was reckless and wrong and yet – and yet Henrietta could not condemn him.

As he clasped her palm to his lips a second time she felt strangely heady, as if champagne bubbles were dancing through her veins.

Her lips parted as she gave an involuntary moan.

She felt him tense at the sound.

His breath hovered on her palm a second longer and then he let go of her hand.

She glanced perplexedly up at him. His features had tightened and his voice conveyed a mocking tone.

"I wonder," he murmured, "if this is the real you?"

Henrietta, brought cruelly back from her moment of self-abandon, repressed a sob.

"The r-real me?"

"Come now," he laughed. "With all the powder and paint removed by your companion's ministrations, I might add – you do look again like the girl I met in the courtyard. Harrietta Reed. I ask again – is this the real *you*?"

What could Henrietta say? It was too late to reveal her true identity. So she nodded miserably.

The Duke remained silent, struggling against some instinct not to say the words he was about to say.

Yet say them he did.

"Miss Reed has many suitors, I hear," he muttered.

"S-she does?"

The Duke's eyes had fixed on her lips.

"Could I but know how many mouths have been venturing there," he sighed abstractedly.

Henrietta was appalled. What tales about her were circulating and engendered by whom?

"You are thinking of – Eddie?" she probed.

"Mr. Bragg! For one, yes," the Duke snorted.

"*For one?*" Henrietta's voice rose in indignation.

Nanny shifted in her chair.

"Hush, hush," he gestured to Henrietta.

"How can I hush, Y-Your Grace, when you impugn me in such a manner?"

The Duke clenched his hand and then relaxed it.

"Forgive me. It's just that it troubles me that I am so torn. I do not know who or what to believe regarding your nature. There is so much I wish to learn about you."

"There is nothing of i-interest to learn. I have been in America for some years w-working with the o-orchestra and am now returning to – to – "

"To seek your fortune perhaps?" he suggested drily. "A husband, an estate?"

Tears stung Henrietta's eyes.

First the Duke was kissing her palm, then he was insulting her! He obviously struggled with his interest in

121

mere *Harrietta Reed*, finding such interest demeaning to his status.

"I d-don't need a fortune!" she blurted out. "I have my own."

A shadow crossed the Duke's forehead.

"Not garnered from playing the piano, I'll warrant."

"W-what do you mean?"

The Duke shrugged and turned away from the bed.

She sat upright to look for her dressing gown and saw with misgiving that it was draped over a nearby chaise.

Glancing at the Duke, she slipped her feet out from under the covers and felt for the steps by her bed.

He turned back and saw her, poised there on the top step, as if trapped in the flare from his eyes.

Her shift was thin and could not disguise the lithe curves of her body, the outline of her breasts, the thrust of her hips. Her hair fell in a blonde sweep to her waist and her colour was high under the Duke's roving scrutiny.

"What do you seek?" he asked, his lips twitching.

"M-my dressing gown," she pointed.

He fetched her gown and held it open before her.

"Put out your arms," he ordered and reached across her and helped her slip her left arm into its sleeve. Then he reached a hand behind, drawing her gown along her back so that her right arm could find the other sleeve.

The Duke's face was so close to her own that their breaths mingled. For an instant his lips came tantalisingly close to hers. Then he seemed to admonish himself, for he drew suddenly back.

"There. You are respectably garbed. *For once.*"

Stung, she watched the Duke move to the window and stoop to pick up the green dress and lay it over a chair.

"Y-Your Grace?"

"Yes?"

"H-how did you know – I was in the maze?"

The Duke's features softened as he remembered.

"I heard your sobs from afar. I was worried when you fell silent."

"And how were you able to find me? Do you know the intricacies of the maze so well?"

"I had not been in the maze since I was a boy. But was led to you by this."

He drew from his pocket a portion of black flounce.

"I used the torn pieces to prevent me going over my tracks," explained Henrietta.

"Most ingenious."

He ran it through his fingers as he surveyed her.

"Tell me, Miss Reed, where will you be lodging in London?"

"I d-don't know. We have not yet decided."

"Surely Mr. Bragg has seen to it that lodgings are secured for his players?"

Henrietta did not know what to say to this.

"There is no relationship between Mr. Bragg and me," she responded at last, "that would make it incumbent upon him to be responsible for my welfare."

The Duke's eyes flashed.

"In that case, Miss Reed, allow me to put at your disposal a house of mine in Bloomsbury."

"A h-house of yours?" Henrietta was taken aback.

"It is not the largest of my properties, but I am sure it will suit you. Until you can find something of your own. I am often in London and will be able to visit you."

Henrietta's eyes widened.

"You would visit there w-with Miss Foss?"

"Miss Foss?" the Duke exploded. "Why on earth would I bring Miss Foss?"

How much more might have been discovered there and then would never be known, for at that moment Nanny started up from her chair and stared dazedly about her.

"What is – happening? *Henrietta*?"

Henrietta's heart leapt into her mouth. Nanny had called out her real name! Had the Duke noticed?

She could not be sure and must despatch him from the room before Nanny could reveal any other details.

She hurried over to Nanny.

"Y-yes, Your Grace, thank you, that would be most convenient for us," she cried over her shoulder. "Perhaps we can discuss it later, for now I must tend to Mrs. Poody – her heart is not good."

"My apologies," the Duke murmured and moved to the door and as he opened it, he turned to glance back.

"I will anticipate our next encounter with pleasure," he bowed and then he was gone.

Nanny regarded Henrietta with a puzzled frown.

"What was that you said about my heart?"

"Oh, Nanny, it was nothing, nothing."

Henrietta kissed her on the cheek and then flung her arms about her, as if to reassure herself that there was one fixed point in her increasingly turbulent universe.

"You seem to have recovered at any rate," muttered Nanny, pleased at this affectionate attention.

Henrietta did not feel recovered at all. She felt full of a strange fever, her thoughts tumbling in her head, her blood roused in her veins.

There was no doubting the source of this sickness.

It lay in the Duke's gaze, his touch, his attention, though of all these were illicit.

Henrietta felt a sob rise in her throat.

With every fibre of her being she longed to feel the Duke's lips again on her all too ardent flesh.

*

It seemed an endless night.

Henrietta tossed and turned under the quilt, finally throwing it from her.

The chimes of the distant clock sounded. Each note struck in tandem with a beat of her heart.

One, two, three – the Duke had left her soon after three – four. Four o'clock.

Her head throbbed and her throat was parched.

She fell back, clutching the damp sheets to her. A moment ago she was too hot. Now she felt chill.

"N-Nanny," she moaned out and then as her senses started to swim, "J-Joe."

Joe! Why had she called for Joe? Joe did not exist. There was no Joe, there was no Harrietta. Alas, for *they* might easily have forged a bond. The head groom and the piano player – were they not of a more or less equal status?

"Joe, I am so thirsty," groaned Henrietta.

There should have been a pitcher of water on her bedside table, but there was none.

She seemed to swim in and out of consciousness, and then her eyes were open as she heard another chime.

Half past four.

The urge to drink was now stronger than her sense of fatigue. With a great effort she swung her legs over the side of the bed. Missing the steps, she slid to the floor.

She hauled herself to her feet and staggered to the door of Nanny's room. Nanny's bed was empty, but she did not see that Nanny was asleep on the couch.

Henrietta turned away, her mind muddled.

She must find Nanny to fetch her a drink of water. Nanny would fetch Joe and Joe would hitch up the wagon. They would all travel to Lushwood together.

She staggered to the door, opened it and peered out along the silent corridor.

Then she stepped out.

In her delirium, she was now home at Lushwood, each door the door of a room she remembered.

She almost floated along the corridor and across the landing at the top of the silent staircase.

Henrietta glided into the corridor of the South wing and paused outside a nail studded oak door.

Mama's room!

She turned the handle and sailed in.

A nightlight burned beside the bed, but the rest of the room was in shadow. A form lay curled under the red counterpane.

On a table at the foot of the bed stood a pitcher of water and a glass.

Henrietta crossed the room eagerly, stumbling into a chair and knocking it clean over as she did so.

"What on earth!"

The form in the bed sat upright with a jolt. Bedcap askew, grey hair instead of black protruding from under its brim, it was no wonder that she did not instantly recognise *Lady Butterclere*.

Instead she pointed at the pitcher of water.

"I-I want a d-drink," she explained disingenuously.

"A likely story!" roared Lady Butterclere, thrusting her feet out of bed and fumbling for her dressing gown. "I know what you were up to, my girl. You've blundered into *my* room, but you were looking for the Duke."

"Joe," mumbled Henrietta, a strange blur forming before her eyes.

"Oh, *Joe*, is it? It's got that far, has it?"

Lady Butterclere, her dressing gown belt trailing on the ground, came looming at Henrietta.

"You wretched, wretched creature," she hissed into her face. "I shall see that you are ruined for this."

"R-ruined?" repeated Henrietta dazedly.

"Ruined, ruined, one thousand times over," intoned Lady Butterclere, reaching for the servants' bell.

She gave it such a vigorous tug that the cord almost came away in her hand.

"What is it, just what is the matter?"

Romany came rushing into the room.

"What's *she* doing here?" she gaped.

"Just wait till I tell you," sneered Lady Butterclere.

Henrietta could hear her through a haze. Her mind wandered and she thought again of Nanny.

"I m-must go," she moaned, turning to the door.

"Oh, no you don't!"

Lady Butterclere caught hold of her by the elbow and, steering her to a chair, pushed her firmly down.

When she tried to rise, Lady Butterclere whipped the belt off her dressing gown and, teeth tightly gritted, tied Henrietta's wrists to the wooden arms.

Romany's eyes grew wide.

"I say – isn't that rather excessive?"

"You think so?" Lady Butterclere rounded on her with an air of triumph. "What do you think she was up to? She was looking for the Duke's chamber, that's what. In her nightdress! And when I caught her, her only excuse was that she was looking for a drink of water!"

"Scandalous!" exploded Romany.

Casting around her furiously, she saw the pitcher of water and took it up.

"There! There's water for you," she cried, tossing its contents fully into Henrietta's face.

Henrietta, utterly bewildered, gazed up at Romany through dripping curls.

"*What is going on here?*"

The Duke, his features twisted in rage, towered at the door.

"Your Grace!"

Lady Butterclere, bobbing a quick curtsy, gestured to Romany to remain silent.

"I had to bind Miss Reed and then dash water into her face to quell her! She was in such a wild fury after I apprehended her in her efforts to find your chamber. I did not summon you, as I wished to spare you the spectacle."

The Duke brushed Lady Butterclere to one side and strode over to Henrietta. Her head lolled now, strands of wet hair falling over her face.

The Duke clenched his jaw.

"Untie her!" he commanded.

"Well, of course, if you insist." Lady Butterclere hastened to loosen the belt about Henrietta's wrists.

"Though to my mind she should be chastised – "

"Should she indeed," replied the Duke, helping the freed Henrietta to her feet.

"And then sent packing," insisted Lady Butterclere. "She is a – a gold digger. You do not see that."

"I see that she is ill," said the Duke grimly, pressing a hand to Henrietta's forehead.

Lady Butterclere pursed her lips.

"Not so ill that she could just wander half-clad about the corridors! Suppose she had blundered into the wing where the Prince of Wales sleeps? You just imagine the scandal! And stepbrother, do you not ask yourself, *why*? What intention had she other than seduction? And who was her quarry, dear stepbrother, if not you? *Who*?"

The Duke wavered. His shoulders sagged and his hand dropped to his side.

When he saw a maid, summoned by the bell, appear anxiously in the doorway, he beckoned her wearily over.

"Would you please escort Miss Reed here back to her room," he ordered.

The maid took her arm and led her away. Henrietta cast a beseeching and bewildered glance at the Duke as she was hurried by, but he had turned his face away.

"I did believe you would see sense," crowed Lady Butterclere with barely concealed triumph.

The Duke turned for a moment to look at Henrietta as she disappeared through the door.

"Nevertheless, we will summon the doctor in the morning," he insisted.

"Oh, it won't be necessary, I assure you," chimed in Lady Butterclere. "She will recover quick enough when she realises how she is exposed. Lord, stepbrother, you are a real innocent in the matter of young women. You should have seen how she carried on aboard *The Boston Queen*."

Henrietta, propelled along the corridor by the maid, heard these words fade out behind her, but could make no sense of them in her fevered condition.

"What's up, Harrie?"

Eddie, en route to his room after a long card game in the servants hall, narrowed his eyes with concern at the sight that approached him.

"I'm ordered to take her to her bed, sir," gloated the maid. "She's been a bad girl."

Eddie put a hand under Henrietta's chin and lifted her now lolling head.

"Harrie?" he questioned with concern.

"F-find P-Poody," was all Henrietta could reply.

"I'll take her from here, thank you." Eddie waved his hand at the maid.

"But I was *ordered*!" spluttered the maid.

"Well, I'm ordering different!"

Eddie encircled Henrietta's tiny waist with his arm, and carried her down the corridor towards the West wing.

Nanny came bursting through from her room when she heard Eddie kick open Henrietta's door.

"I woke up and found her gone!" she cried, rushing tearfully towards them. "Where has she been?"

"I'm not rightly sure, Mrs. Poody."

Nanny put a hand to Henrietta's brow.

"She's feverish!" she exclaimed.

"She doesn't seem herself at all," agreed Eddie.

"I'll get her into bed now and in the morning – I'll have a doctor fetched."

Eddie looked unhappy.

"The orchestra is due to leave Merebury tomorrow. I know she's not going to be performing with us again, but I'd sure hate to leave her behind. I don't know, but I feel there's some ill wind blowing in this place."

Nanny was too busy settling Henrietta into bed to hear Eddie's last sentence.

"If you have to leave without us, then so be it," she said. "Although I would have preferred to travel with you all. It has been such fun."

Eddie gave one rueful glance back and departed.

*

It was five o'clock in the morning, and seven, and eight – each chime coming faintly to Henrietta's ear.

It was day, but the moon did not go away. It came right in the window to hover over her bed. Only it had a ruddy face and it spoke.

It felt her pulse and put a stethoscope to her breast and shook its head.

"*Tut tut,*" the moon gurgled.

It shook a bottle and poured liquid into a spoon that was held at her lips and the liquid trickled down her throat.

After that, she slept and slept and slept.

She did not see the faces of Eddie and Kitty loom briefly over her to murmur goodbye nor hear the rumble of wheels lurching off for the station at Liverpool.

She did not hear, later, the ceremonious departure of the Prince of Wales and his retinue.

She did not register the deep silence that seemed to settle over Merebury, nor the sky growing ever blacker.

Only once did she swim into consciousness, and it was then she glimpsed a tall figure standing with his elbow on the mantelpiece, staring gloomily into the fire.

"Joe?" she wondered aloud, but the sudden dash of hail against the casement window drowned her frail voice and the figure at the mantelpiece never turned his head.

CHAPTER NINE

All that night and during the following day, a storm raged without.

The wind howling down the chimney sounded like hungry wolves. The draught fanned the fire and shadowy flames danced madly on the ceiling.

Henrietta drifted in and out of consciousness. The doctor said that her nerves must indeed have been stretched to breaking point for her to succumb so totally to the fever.

"Rest will cure her sooner than my medicines," he prognosticated.

Sure enough by evening, her temperature somewhat abated. She was able to sit up in bed and take a little broth.

Nanny blamed herself for ever allowing Henrietta to come to Merebury with the orchestra.

"It's all been too much for you," she sighed,

"It doesn't matter, Nanny," she murmured, her eyes closed. "It's been a-an experience."

"An experience that has made you ill!"

"I'll soon be well again, Nanny, and then we'll set off for London."

"The sooner the better," grumbled Nanny.

She was growing increasingly uneasy at Merebury and did not want to tell Henrietta the reason, which was that Prince Vasily was now a guest here himself!

He had visited Lady Butterclere and her *protégée*

yesterday, the day after the ball and when the weather grew stormy he was invited to stay the night.

"Have you finished that broth, my dear?"

"Y-yes, Nanny."

"I'll take the tray down myself. That little maid we have takes an age to answer the bell and then she always has an insolent air on her little pug face."

She felt Nanny lift the tray and heard her hasten to the door. There was the squeak of the hinge and then low voices before the door was gently closed.

Someone had entered the room, however, as Nanny exited, as footsteps were crossing the room towards her.

After a long silence, Henrietta opened drowsy eyes.

There stood the Duke, his arms outstretched so that either hand rested on each of the two lower canopy posts.

"Mrs. Poody said you took some broth."

"Y-yes, Your Grace."

She had only a hazy memory of their last encounter, but she recalled that it had not been a happy one and was therefore perplexed to see him in her room.

Perhaps he wished to check on her progress, eager to have her away from Merebury and out of his life!

"I – am sure I shall be well enough to leave soon."

"Please do not think that is a prospect I anticipate with any great pleasure, Miss Reed."

Henrietta's pale brow creased wonderingly.

The Duke ran a hand through his hair.

"Last night," he now began, "I did you a disservice, Miss Reed. I did allow myself to be persuaded that your nocturnal wandering was not for innocent reasons."

Henrietta made as if to speak, but the Duke held up a silencing hand.

"I have come tonight to apologise for my error and to make it clear that the offer of my house in London still stands. I have already written to inform the servants that you and Mrs. Poody will be arriving sometime this week – depending of course on your state of health."

His gaze travelled from her eyes to her lips and then he suddenly turned violently away.

"Good God, if I could be but sure – "

"S-sure – Your Grace?"

"Nothing. I am babbling, Miss Reed. Put it down to the trials and tribulations of throwing a ball. Followed by grave concern over the health of an esteemed guest."

He strode to her side and lifted her hand to his lips.

"Now let me bid you goodnight. Sweet Harrietta."

As she felt the Duke's mouth on her skin, she gave a shudder.

He lifted his head and regarded her with dismay.

"You are still so feverish?"

She wondered that he did not read the yearning in her eyes.

"N-no, Your Grace. Just – a little chill."

The Duke stood for a moment, clasping her hand. Their eyes locked and their mutual breath became as one.

The window rattled at the mercy of a force without that seemed to echo the force they felt within – the force that rises mercilessly in unguarded breasts and threatens to overthrow the stoutest heart.

The Duke's grip tightened. It was as if he wished to crush Henrietta's fingers to powder.

Her eyelids fluttered and a moan of ecstasy escaped her lips.

"Oh, God," groaned the Duke.

He ripped his hand away, letting her own hand drop heavily onto the counterpane and strode to the door.

"Get well, Miss Reed," he called huskily. "Get well and go to London. There we may develop this intercourse away from prying eyes and insinuating tongues."

The door closed heavily behind him.

Henrietta's heart took some minutes to return to its regular beat.

It was still racing when Nanny came in with grapes and a glass of hot lemon and sugar.

She propped herself up and gazed at the dancing fire. She could feel the pulse in her neck throbbing wildly.

"You're still looking rather flushed, my dear," said Nanny worriedly.

"It's nothing, the heat of the fire – that is all. Why don't you go and lie down for a while now. I am fine."

Nanny left her reluctantly and she snuggled against the pillows and stared dreamily ahead.

The Duke had reiterated the offer of his house in London and she and Nanny could stay there for a few days before venturing on to Lushwood, although she wondered how easy it would be for her to remain Harrietta Reed in a City where so many knew her as Henrietta Radford.

The idea that the Duke would come and visit her was exciting beyond measure.

Yet it did not seem quite right for him to suggest it. He had seemed surprised, almost outraged, when she had enquired if Miss Foss would accompany him.

Did he intend to travel alone and did he intend his visits to be secret? If so, why?

And what did he mean when he mentioned '*prying eyes and insinuating tongues*?'

The casement window rattled again. In the hearth coals sizzled loudly as rain was blown down the chimney.

She shivered and drew the counterpane to her chin.

The door to her room creaked as it slowly opened and she could not see at first who had entered, although she heard footsteps cross the room.

Two figures came into view at the end of the bed.

It was Lady Butterclere with the pug-faced maid, grinning just like a malicious monkey behind the quivering bulk of her mistress.

Lady Butterclere's eyes were slits of fury.

"What does this mean?" she screeched.

Henrietta was bewildered.

"W-what does what mean?"

"This, this!"

Lady Butterclere tapped a letter that lay folded on her palm.

"I d-don't know. What is it?"

"*What is it, what is it?*" mocked the maid. "Lawks, your Ladyship, isn't she a dizzembler. I'm glad I had the sense to deliver it to *you* and not to *her*."

"Be quiet," snapped Lady Butterclere.

"You don't know what is written here?" she waved the letter at Henrietta.

"H-how can I? I have not even seen it until now."

Lady Butterclere shook the letter open and began to read aloud.

"*Dear Miss Reed, here is the address of my London property. The servants will endeavour to make your stay as comfortable as possible. I look forward to calling upon you as soon as I am able to travel to London. Meanwhile, I am at your devoted service until you leave Merebury.*"

Lady Butterclere's eyes almost bulged with outrage from their sockets as she went on,

"Yes, and there it is, written down as bold as brass. *40 Manchester Square.* All the beds made up and all the silver polished for the arrival of the Duke's *hussy!*"

Henrietta's head swam.

"H-hussy?"

Lady Butterclere sneered.

"What else did you think you would be? His wife? Surely you just cannot be so naïve as to be unaware of the significance of the Duke's offer? Manchester Square, my dear, is where he keeps his mistresses. And you are to be the next. For as long as you keep his interest, that is."

Henrietta gripped the counterpane tight.

"M-mistress? I don't believe that is his intention."

Lady Butterclere's lip curled.

"Really? Did he not suggest that his fiancée would join him when he called on you? Answer me. Did he?"

Henrietta shook her head numbly.

"There you are!" Lady Butterclere almost reared up in triumph. "What can that mean but that he intends to keep his visits to you a secret? And why would he do that if his intentions were honourable?

"His intentions towards Miss Foss are *honourable.* She is the one he will marry and she is the one who will be the next Duchess of Merebury!

"You, my dear, are to be a dirty little secret tucked away behind lowered blinds in a fancy square. And when he is right through with you, you will have neither home nor reputation left!"

Henrietta listened with mounting horror, shrinking under Lady Butterclere's baleful eye. Would nothing stem this poisonous flow?

"You thought you could get him to renounce Miss Foss in your favour, but you were wrong. He would never sully the family name by marrying beneath him. And I am going to make sure that you do not distract his amorous attentions from his fiancée for one second more.

"If you so much as set one foot in that house in Manchester Square, I will destroy you utterly. I shall see to it that you are shunned and spat at in the street!"

"*No more*. No more. Go away," moaned Henrietta, pressing her hands to her ears.

Lady Butterclere paused and drew herself up with grim satisfaction.

"That's *you* done for, Miss Reed," she hissed.

She glided over to the door and stood waiting for the maid to open it. The maid smirked at Henrietta as Lady Butterclere sailed through and slammed the door after her.

"What is all this rumpus?"

Nanny stumbled half asleep from her room.

Henrietta could not speak. Her breast heaved with sobs though no sound came from her lips.

"Henrietta, what is it?" Nanny asked fearfully.

At last her voice emerged in a wail of grief.

"I c-cannot stay h-here another hour, Nanny, we m-must pack."

"Pack? Tonight?"

Tears streamed unchecked down her pale cheeks.

"Y-yes. T-tonight," she insisted.

"Henrietta, you are delirious again!"

"N-no, Nanny. My mind is most clear. I must leave tonight or I shall d-die of shame."

"But, my dear, what can have driven you to this?"

She could make no sense of Henrietta's reply, for the girl's words were lost in a welter of sobs.

Nanny tried to touch her forehead, but she brushed away her hand, her breast heaving more violently yet.

"All right. Sssh, now. Sshh." Nanny was thinking frantically. "I'll start packing. But have you thought about how we shall travel at this hour?"

"N-no."

"I must go and ask the Duke for a coach."

"*NO!*"

Nanny gaped at this fierce response.

"But why not, pray?"

"Not the Duke. You must *not* ask him. Ask Lady Butterclere,"

"Lady Butterclere?"

"Yes."

Henrietta's tone was very bitter.

"She will be only too glad to see the back of us."

It was this bitterness that decided Nanny. It was paramount that she take her charge away from Merebury, before she suffered a complete nervous collapse.

"Put something warm on, my dear. I am going to speak to Lady Butterclere. I will be back as soon as I can."

Henrietta wrapped herself in the counterpane and curled her legs up under her as the tears flowed.

The Duke had dropped the bait and reeled her in. How willingly she had agreed to stay in his London house.

How unwittingly she had acceded to his nefarious designs. No doubt he would have come to the house and there he would have mercilessly ravished her.

Henrietta buried her head on her knees.

The worst aspect of this was she could not be sure that she would not have welcomed his illicit embrace. Had she not thrilled already to his touch, although he was sworn to another?

An hour passed before Nanny's breathless return.

"Lady Butterclere has agreed to order a coach and four horses to be hitched up," she panted. "And she has found a coachman prepared to take us as far as Liverpool."

"W-who might that be?"

"How should I know?" Nanny was becoming tired and cross. "I wish I knew what all this is about. Sneaking off late at night like this. And Lady Butterclere insisting we tell no one, least of all the Duke. It's not courteous, so it's not. I must be mad to allow myself to be dragged out into that howling night."

Nanny started the packing while Henrietta dressed lethargically.

They froze when a knock came at the door, but it was only two footmen for their luggage.

Once the room was cleared Nanny took a final look round and then straightened Henrietta's hood.

"Well, here we go, missy," she said in a low voice, "slipping away like two thieves in the night."

In the cobbled courtyard, the horses jerked at their bridles uneasily. Even they seemed to sense the strangeness of this journey.

The coach driver in oilskins against the inclement weather, a hat low on his forehead, growled a greeting and held open the door.

He gave a hand to Nanny, who climbed in first and then he aided Henrietta. She did not look at him as she stepped up. He closed the door firmly behind her.

Barely had she settled herself when a familiar voice from the darkness outside stopped her heart.

"What is happening? Who ordered this coach?"

The coachman answered in a low voice,

"Why, the two ladies within."

The Duke wrenched open the door.

"Mrs. Poody and – Miss Reed!" he exclaimed.

Henrietta shrank back from his stunned gaze.

"What – are you fleeing my hospitality?"

Henrietta, her heart in her mouth, could not speak. She merely gave a frightened nod.

The Duke's eyes narrowed.

He turned to Nanny.

"Mrs. Poody, perhaps *you* will be so kind as to tell me what is going on?"

Nanny threw up her hands.

"I can't. I know nothing. I'm that put out by it all, but I must do as Hen – Miss Reed wishes."

He turned back to Henrietta, a slow blaze beginning to burn in his eyes.

"Miss Reed – explain yourself at once or get out of this carriage immediately," he said through gritted teeth.

"N-no," whispered Henrietta.

The Duke reached a hand in and caught her arm.

"By God, you will get out at once and tell me what madness makes you steal away from my home like this."

She tore herself violently from the Duke's hold. He stepped back, astonished at her vehemence.

"Coachman," Henrietta cried, "drive on, please."

The Duke whirled round and raised a hand to the coachman.

"Do not on any account obey, sir. Remember, you answer to me."

141

The coachman gave a low chuckle.

"Oh no, Your Grace, tonight I answer to the lady. Tomorrow, though, *she* answers to *me*."

"What the devil do you mean and who are you?"

The coachman leaped onto his box as he replied,

"I mean that henceforth Miss Reed belongs to me. *Prince Vasily* – who is otherwise at your service."

Before the Duke could respond or Henrietta inside the carriage cry out in dawning horror, the whip whistled through the air and the horses darted forward.

The coach and its occupants spun from the cobbled courtyard and onto the muddied road.

*

"*Harrie! Harrie!*"

Henrietta stirred as a voice murmured in her ear.

"*Harrie*? Wake up!"

Henrietta's eyelids fluttered open and she gazed in amazement and utter relief at the face leaning over her.

"*Kitty*! Oh, Kitty. I am so glad to see you. But what on earth are you doing here?"

"I might well ask you the same thing."

Henrietta glanced at the gloomy room she found herself in and threw her hands over her face in despair.

How Nanny and she had clutched at each other in terror last night as the coach had hurtled on its way!

She could have wept at her folly. Why had she not waited until the morning to leave Merebury? She might by then have confronted the Duke and demanded a carriage.

She should never have trusted Lady Butterclere.

Nanny had told her, as they lurched on through the dark countryside, that Prince Vasily had been visiting Lady Butterclere's apartments regularly in the last two days.

No doubt Lady Butterclere considered it a coup to engage the services of the Prince in whisking her away in the middle of the night – her reputation would be damaged beyond repair once it was known she had gone with him.

The coach had bumped over potholes and lurched through dripping woods, Prince Vasily thrashing the whip like a madman.

He obviously had a goal in mind.

Sure enough, just after midnight, the coach turned in under a decrepit stone arch and drew up outside a mean-looking thatched inn.

Prince Vasily scrambled from the box and opened the carriage door.

"Our lodgings for the night," he leered.

Gingerly Nanny and Henrietta descended and a fat man with a lantern led them into the inn.

A few twigs spat in the hearth. Nanny sank onto a bench and closed her eyes – the latest turn of events had exhausted her old frame utterly.

This inn had been, it seemed, the lodgings of Prince Vasily for the last few days, though he had spent last night at Merebury. The fat man was the landlord.

"No other guest has arrived since I was away, eh?" asked the Prince, looking round warily.

"Just one couple," shrugged the fat man.

"That I do not like," frowned the Prince.

"That *I* do not like," grunted the landlord, pointing at Henrietta and Nanny. "Especially as I've yet to see the colour of your money."

The Prince thrust Henrietta forward into the light.

"There is the colour of my money," he cried.

The landlord surveyed Henrietta with interest.

"Kidnapped her, 'ave you?"

"Yes. Yes, he has!" she cried out. "And I demand you fetch the authorities."

"What, on a night like this? Not me, 'sides, I never come between a man and his paramour."

"I am *not* his paramour!"

But the landlord had turned away.

"Her and the old lady will have to take a room up in the attic," he said to the Prince.

"Good," nodded Prince Vasily.

He stared at Henrietta for just a moment, his tongue running over his upper lip, and then he shrugged,

"Let her remain a maiden – one more night! But tomorrow, you will find me a priest, eh, landlord?"

"If it stops raining. Maybe," he replied.

Holding the lantern high, he gestured to Henrietta and Nanny to follow him.

Henrietta was too frightened by what the Prince had intimated was to be her fate and Nanny too tired to make any protest at the dingy quarters he ushered them into.

They had both fallen asleep exhausted in no time.

"Harrie!" came Kitty's voice suddenly. "You need to listen to me."

Henrietta woke up and stared at Kitty, who sat on the edge of the bed and in a whisper – as Nanny still slept – quickly explained how she herself came to be at the inn.

The orchestra had set out together in their various conveyances, but Kitty and Trescot, travelling at the back, had fallen behind.

The weather became increasingly stormy towards evening and one of the wheels flew off their carriage and they were almost toppled into a ditch.

The driver unhitched the two horses and led Kitty and Trescot to the nearest inhabited abode – the inn.

Prince Vasily was not there that evening as he had gone to Merebury and been invited by Lady Butterclere to stay when the weather turned threatening.

They took a room at the inn and their driver rode off to find a wheelwright.

"But you know," continued Kitty, "we were waiting all day yesterday, with the endless wind and rain, and then we had to spend tonight here too.

"The landlord got very chatty over supper and kept telling us about this foreign Prince who was lodging here, but the idea seemed preposterous. To tell you the truth, we didn't believe him.

"Anyway, we got to bed early, but I was awakened in the early hours by the sound of a coach. I recognised your voice and some instinct made me listen."

Henrietta's eyes filled with tears.

"Then you heard it all? All that the Prince intends?"

Kitty nodded grimly.

"I heard the rat all right. But don't worry, Harrie. The Prince and that tub of butter the landlord drank a lot of wine and are asleep till doomsday, as far as I can see.

"Trescot crept down to the stable and has harnessed up the coach you arrived in. Your baggage is still on it. It will take us all out of here and he won't be able to follow."

"Oh, Kitty. How can I ever repay you?"

"There's no time for that kind of talk, until I can get that skunk in front of the authorities – "

Kitty broke off in surprise as Henrietta caught hold of her sleeve.

"No!" whispered Henrietta fervently. "Tell no one.

Promise me. If you do, they will want Miss Reed to appear in court. And – that just cannot happen. Please, Kitty, get us to the – nearest railway station."

"I just don't understand, but I'll do what you ask," sighed Kitty. "Now are you ready?"

Henrietta woke Nanny who was befuddled at first to see Kitty, but soon understood what she must do.

The three now filed carefully along the corridor and down the stairs. The snores of the Prince and the landlord rang from behind closed doors.

Trescot was waiting. He opened the carriage door, the ladies stepped in and he climbed onto the box.

With a jerk of the reins, the coach rumbled away.

Leaning against Nanny, Henrietta hugged her cape joyfully around her.

She would not allow all that had happened with the Duke and with Prince Vasily to sour this moment.

With every hoof beat, each turn of the wheels, she was leaving Miss Reed and her mishaps behind.

Ahead lay her home.

Ahead lay reunion with her dear father.

And ahead lay the most important thing of all.

Reunion with her own true self – Henrietta Radford of Lushwood Manor, Hertfordshire.

CHAPTER TEN

It was early morning and Henrietta threw open her bedroom window, leaned on the sill and surveyed the dew-bright gardens below.

She had been home at Lushwood for two months by now and this was her happiest hour, when she least felt the shadow of recent events hovering over her.

At least she had not set eyes on Prince Vasily again. He could not pursue Henrietta Radford after her return to Society, for he was a wanted man in England.

She supposed he had since shipped himself off to the safety of Europe.

Kitty, now appraised of Miss Reed's true identity by Eddie, had written once.

Eddie's regular pianist had finally arrived for what turned out to be a highly successful tour of England.

She had heard nothing of the Duke, his stepsister or Romany Foss.

There had been much to do at Lushwood and that, plus the return of her father from America, had prevented her from brooding too much on her feelings for the Duke.

"Henrietta?"

Lord Radford appeared, waving a letter at her.

"Lady Bridgely is holding a ball next week and we are both invited to Castle Bridgely!"

Henrietta paled.

Her father knew nothing of her escapade with the Eddie Bragg orchestra. Nanny had sworn never to mention it and had anyway returned to live in her own cottage.

She now hoped that the distance between the Duke and herself would ensure their worlds never collided.

Any invitation, however, was a potential threat.

"Where is Bridgely, Papa? It isn't up North, is it?"

"No, child. It's in Hampshire. Not too far away."

Lord Radford waited expectantly.

"We must go then, Papa, mustn't we?" she replied reluctantly.

"Excellent!" agreed her father and hurried out.

Henrietta turned again to the window. Two white doves were cooing softly to each other on the sill.

How she wished her own heart might feel as joyous and full of song as theirs.

*

"You have been hiding this treasure away for too long, you naughty man!" Lady Bridgely reprimanded Lord Radford as her scrutiny took in the figure of his daughter.

Henrietta blushed.

She had no idea how bewitching she looked. She just seemed to shimmer in her dress of rose-coloured silk overlain with sequined gauze.

Many heads turned as she and her father now stood conversing in the ballroom with their hostess.

"She will certainly not be short of dancing partners. By the way we have engaged a superb orchestra," added Lady Bridgely. "They played on *The Boston Queen*."

"The Eddie Bragg Orchestra is here?"

"Yes."

"I shall be so very thrilled to see them – hear them again," cried Henrietta.

"They were strongly recommended by my cousin," explained Lady Bridgley. "You will be pleased to hear, Lord Radford, that my cousin will attend us this evening."

"Oh, what a delight!" exclaimed Lord Radford.

He smiled at Henrietta as Lady Bridgely made her excuses and moved off to greet other guests.

"Her cousin would often visit us at Lushwood when your grandfather was alive. Why, you danced with him one night in the hallway – in your nightdress, too!"

Henrietta was astonished.

"How did you know about that?"

"He told your mother and me!" her father laughed. "Said you had totally enchanted him. How I shall relish introducing the Duke to you again after all these years."

"H-he is a Duke?" asked Henrietta in a low voice.

"That's right, my dear. *The Duke of Merebury*."

Henrietta felt faint.

No wonder she had been mysteriously drawn to the Duke when she thought she did not know him.

No wonder she had formed an image of him that had turned out to be uncannily similar to the real man.

Henrietta swallowed.

"Papa – I don't want to be introduced to the Duke."

Lord Radford looked at his daughter in amazement.

"Why on earth not?"

Henrietta cast around desperately for an answer.

"I have heard that he has become – a terrible roué."

" A *roué*?"

149

"Y-yes, Papa. He – keeps mistresses in his house in M-Manchester Square."

"Henrietta, who has been spreading this rumour?"

"A-a fellow passenger on board *The Boston Queen*. Lady B-Butterclere."

"The Duke's stepsister? You have mistaken her, my dear. She must have been referring to the Duke's late grandfather. Now *he* was notorious. But there has never been any such scandal or tittle-tattle attached to the name of the present Duke."

"B-but Lady Butterclere was most precise, Papa."

"Then she was stirring up mischief. I must admit, I never did like her on the few occasions I met her – "

She might have learned a good lot more about Lady Butterclere at that moment had she not been distracted by the sound of her name called out with evident delight.

Kitty came rushing towards her from the middle of the crowd in the ballroom.

"Harrie, Harrie, is it really you?" trilled Kitty.

"*Harrie*?" repeated Lord Radford in surprise.

Henrietta, feeling flustered now introduced Kitty as another fellow passenger from *The Boston Queen*.

"She calls me Harrie as a nickname, Papa. Because on board she knew me as Harrietta."

"Ah!" exhaled Lord Radford.

Kitty gave Lord Radford a flirtatious curtsy.

"I'm very pleased to meet you, sir! And I apologise for calling your daughter by such a silly name. But do you mind if I whisk her away from you? We've much news to catch up on."

"Be my guest," Lord Radford twinkled.

Henrietta wanted to reiterate to him the plea that he not effect an introduction to the Duke, but Kitty took such a firm grip of her elbow and steered her so forcibly away that Lord Radford was quickly left behind.

Kitty propelled her to a sofa and they sat down.

"You'll never guess," she began without ceremony, "who hired us last week to play at a party?"

She leaned in conspiratorially.

"*Lady Butterclere.*"

"Was that at – at Merebury?"

"No. It was in Manchester Square."

Henrietta opened her fan and stared for a moment at its coloured folds.

"Was the D-Duke there?" she asked.

"No. But I'll tell you who was. Prince Vasily."

Henrietta almost dropped the fan.

"V-Vasily? He is still in England?"

"Never left its shores, Harrie. Sorry – Henrietta. I don't know if he came to London looking for *you*, but he's set himself up here. Has the nerve of the devil, too.

"And he was – Lady Butterclere's guest?"

"He seemed more than a guest, Harrie. He hung about Lady Butterclere and Miss Foss all evening."

Kitty lowered her voice still further.

"Apparently the Duke has refused to have him at Merebury. But whenever Lady Butterclere is in London – and that seems to be every other week – she invites Vasily to Manchester Square."

"H-how do you know all this?"

"That pug-faced maid told me. She's convinced the Prince is out to seduce Lady Butterclere since the Duke has settled a large sum upon her and gave her the Manchester Square house. But I think the Prince – "

"*He gave her the house?*"

Henrietta repeated the words in bewilderment.

If the Duke really did use the house in London for assignations, why would he hand it over to his stepsister?

Unless – and the thought made her head swim with horror – *unless Lady Butterclere really had been lying to her all along!*

In which case she had seriously maligned the Duke.

"Harrie? Are you listening to me?"

Henrietta turned an abstracted gaze upon Kitty.

"I-I'm sorry. W-what were you saying?"

"I was saying that Prince Vasily has other designs."

"Oh. I w-wonder how he has managed to e-evade the authorities? After all, he is a wanted man in England."

"Oh, it is rumoured that Lady Butterclere has used her influence to keep him at liberty."

Before Kitty could tell her any more the next guests were loudly announced.

"His Grace the Duke of Merebury, accompanied by Lady Butterclere and Miss Romany Foss."

Henrietta froze.

This was the moment she had been dreading!

The Duke appeared in the doorway.

He was easily the most dashing and distinguished gentleman in the ballroom, though he was paler than usual and his hooded expression strangely grave for the occasion.

Lady Butterclere and Romany Foss stood on either side of him.

Henrietta rubbed her eyes in disbelief – Miss Foss seemed transformed.

Her eyes were shining, her usually ashen features were flushed, her hair was beautifully arranged. She was dressed most elegantly in a gown of midnight blue.

Kitty followed Henrietta's gaze.

"Would you not say, Harrie," she giggled, "that there stands a woman who is head over heels in love?"

She could not tear her agonised gaze from Romany – no woman in love could look that resplendent unless *her love was returned*!

Yet the Duke did not look at his fiancée. His eyes roved the room as if seeking a familiar face, lingering on the orchestra dais and then moving on to the throng below.

In another second, thought Henrietta frantically, he will see me!

She leaped to her feet.

"Wait on, Harrie, you haven't heard everything – " Kitty protested vehemently.

"Later, later," cried Henrietta.

She darted away, swift as a swallow, towards the other side of the ballroom, and into one of the alcoves that were set deep in the wall behind dark red velvet curtains.

She collapsed onto the sofa within and sat fanning her hot cheeks, her heart fluttering violently.

Next it almost nearly stopped beating altogether as she heard the Duke's voice greeting her father just beyond her hiding place.

"A great pleasure to see you again, Lord Radford."

"And it's delightful to see you again, Duke, after all this time," he replied. "You are hardier than I, I must say. I doubt I should have travelled such a great distance for the sake of a ball."

"Well, it is thrown by my cousin, and I was hoping to encounter a familiar face here. But it seems I am to be disappointed."

"Perhaps I can allay some of your disappointment by introducing you to my daughter! I am sure she will be happy to dance with her mysterious stranger again!"

The Duke gave a good-humoured laugh.

"She enchanted me once, Lord Radford, and I have no doubt she will enchant me again!"

"If she might be found – " muttered Lord Radford as they moved out of earshot.

Since it was the Duke who had suggested to Lady Bridgely that she might hire the orchestra, it was obviously *Harrietta Reed* who he hoped to encounter here tonight.

Imagine if he had mentioned that name aloud. Her father would have known who the Duke meant at once.

"I will have to remain secreted here all night," she groaned aloud in despair.

"That, dear lady, will greatly please me," came a voice from the recesses of the alcove.

Henrietta turned with a loud gasp.

Beyond the faint glow of the gas lamp she could just make out the figure of a man sitting in a wing chair.

"P-Prince Vasily," she stammered, blood draining from her cheeks.

"Poor Henrietta," the Prince mocked her. "Caught between, how do you say it? *The devil and the deep blue sea!*"

That phrase had never rung so horribly true as she realised that she was now condemned either to endure the company of the man she hated most in the world, or to be unmasked before the man who, night or day, was never out of her tormented thoughts.

"Twice you have now scorned me, Miss Radford," grated the Prince. "Now it feels good to know I have the power to expose you before Society."

"That w-would – destroy my father."

The Prince shrugged.

"So what is it you will offer me to remain silent?"

Before Henrietta could make a reply – though reply she had none – she heard Kitty's voice calling her.

"*Harrie?*"

Kitty was clearly looking into each alcove by turn and was nearing this very one.

Prince Vasily exclaimed in annoyance.

"Put out that lamp," he hissed.

"W-what?"

"The lamp, damn you, the lamp."

Henrietta rose and extinguished the lamp. Now she alone was visible in the light from the ballroom while the Prince was in utter darkness.

"If she comes in here, send her away," he ordered. "You and I have unfinished business still."

Trembling, Henrietta sat down again.

She had no doubt that if she disobeyed the Prince he would just drag her forth from the alcove and ridicule her before the throng.

'*This young lady has masqueraded as a showgirl and piano player, both on board a ship and at the home of a distinguished aristocrat. She lost the trust of her host the Duke when he discovered her roaming the corridors of his home late at night.*

Subsequently, she fled his hospitality in company with another man. Myself.'

She could never subject her father to such a scene.

Kitty parted the curtain and peered in.

"Harrie! There you are! Why are you in the dark?"

"I h-have a headache."

"Is there anything I can get for you?"

"N-no. I just – would like to be alone."

Undeterred, Kitty entered the alcove and plumped herself down on the sofa beside her.

"Phew, but it's getting hot out there. And I haven't even been dancing. In fact – in fact, I've been chatting to the Duke."

Henrietta felt herself tense up, all too aware of the Prince listening in the darkness.

"Y-you have?"

"Yes. And most melancholy he seemed, asking me where Miss Reed might be. But that's just another story – I still haven't finished telling you everything about Lady Butterclere – "

Her voice trailed away as she stared at Henrietta in the gloom.

"Harrie, are you okay?"

"Yes. Please, tell me what it is you have to tell me and then – go. I'm sorry, but I'm really not feeling well."

"Honey, my news will distract you from all your woes!"

Kitty took a deep breath.

"Remember Eddie saying he was sure he had seen that skinny Lizzie, Miss Foss, before? Well, at the party at Manchester Square, our regular pianist, Louie, sets eyes on Miss Foss and places her immediately.

"Years ago, the orchestra performed at a house in Portland, Oregon. The daughter of the house, Clara, was home on holiday from her finishing school and brought a friend with her and that friend was – Romany Foss."

Despite herself, Henrietta was now listening with interest.

"Clara was a bit talkative, especially when she and Louie were having something of a romantic *tête à tête* in the garden! She revealed that Miss Romany Foss was the illegitimate daughter of an English lady – an aristocrat who resided most of the year in New York!"

"L-Lady B-Butterclere?" gasped Henrietta.

She could feel Prince Vasily tense in the darkness.

"That's right," nodded Kitty. "Seems that after her husband Lord Butterclere died, she went out West to find herself a wealthy husband. She didn't find a husband, but she *did* fall for a smooth talker, but who then disappeared when Lady Butterclere discovered that she was expecting his child.

"She had the child in Portland, fostered it out, then paid over the years for expensive schooling. She rarely visited and kept the whole matter secret.

"Because, of course, she had made big plans for her daughter. Come hell or high water, Lady Butterclere was going to marry her off to her stepbrother back in England!"

Henrietta's hand flew to her mouth.

"The – the Duke!"

"Correct. All her life poor Romany Foss was being primed to marry her own step-uncle. Anyway, Romany is in awe of her mother, and will do most anything she's told. Except she didn't keep her real identity secret."

"W-who did she tell?"

"It was someone who had insinuated himself into her trust. Someone who saw an opportunity for himself in the secret. Someone who recognised that Lady Butterclere would ensure that her daughter was never in want, whether she married the Duke or another.

"Someone who then seduced Miss Foss and made her fall violently in love with him."

"W-who?"

"Can't you guess? Your old friend Prince Vasily," Kitty laughed. "Well, I had better get back to the dance. Hope you have forgotten your headache by now, my dear."

With these words, Kitty swept out of the alcove.

There was silence for a moment.

Prince Vasily was breathing hard in the darkness.

Henrietta felt that she herself might leave too, but as she gathered up her skirts, she felt a restraining hand on her shoulder.

"Did I say, Miss Radford, you may go?"

Henrietta sank back down onto the sofa.

"N-no. But why should you detain me? You have no hold over me now. I know too much about you."

Prince Vasily gave a mocking chuckle.

"You think so? You know about Miss Foss, but as regards me, there is only what this Miss Kitty says. And what is her proof? Observation only."

"M-Miss Foss would bear her out!"

"Miss Foss? She is my creature and she will never betray me. She and I, we will elope and Lady Butterclere will pay us so much money from the Duke's settlement to keep it secret that she ever had an illegitimate child!"

Henrietta swallowed hard, casting a desperate look toward the closed curtain.

"Then what can you want from me?" she asked.

"What I will not enjoy so much when I have it from Romany Foss," whispered Prince Vasily.

His finger ran down Henrietta's neck and then his hand moved to her bodice, flicking at the lace that covered her breast.

Henrietta pushed his hand away.

In one move he cleared the sofa and stood before her leering down.

"You will learn how a man like me can love!"

Henrietta attempted to rise, but he pushed her back, clamping a hand over her mouth so that she could utter no sound.

She struggled as with his other hand he began to lift the skirt of her dress.

Next the curtain was wrenched aside.

Prince Vasily was torn from where he was standing and thrust heavily to the floor.

An enraged Duke of Merebury stood outlined in the light that now flooded the alcove from the ballroom.

A sea of faces – Miss Foss, Lady Butterclere, Kitty, Lady Bridgely – hovered behind him.

The orchestra meanwhile had stopped playing.

"I knew I'd heard someone," said Kitty grimly.

The Duke spoke through gritted teeth.

"Get up, you scoundrel, and take the beating you damn well deserve."

"No! No!"

A weeping Romany Foss rushed forward and flung herself on Prince Vasily as he attempted to rise.

He sank back onto a seated position with Romany clutching his knees.

Lady Butterclere paled.

The Duke took Henrietta's hand in his and drew her gently to her feet.

"You are unscathed?" he enquired.

"Y-yes," she blushed beneath his concerned gaze.

"What is going on?" asked Lord Radford, pushing his way through.

In one glance he understood the scene and turned in dismay to his daughter.

"My God! Are you all right, Henrietta?"

The Duke's gaze flickered.

"Henri – *etta*?"

"Not Miss Reed?" spluttered Lady Butterclere.

Lord Radford started.

"Miss Reed? Oh, that was only the name I invented for her to travel under on *The Boston Queen*. To try and protect her from fortune-hunters."

He threw a contemptuous look at Prince Vasily.

"Her real name is of course Henrietta Radford, who most of you will know as my own dear daughter."

"Your daughter, Lord Radford?" echoed the Duke in surprise.

"Yes. Henrietta, with whom you danced long ago at Lushwood Manor," he smiled.

The Duke stared down at the floor, the muscles in his jaw tightening.

'*Now he knows all,*' thought Henrietta in despair.

Lady Butterclere's features distorted with rage.

All her plans to marry off her daughter to the Duke were now dashed. Romany had made it all too clear her allegiance to the shamed Prince Vasily.

Well, if Romany was not going to have the Duke, neither was that conniving Miss Reed or Miss Radford or whatever she was!

"I had no idea at all that Miss Reed was of such an established family," she began. "Her escapades on board ship were such as to – "

It was the Duke who cut in, lifting his head quickly.

"Madam, I suggest you would be better employed removing your friend from the scene to compose herself."

At these words Romany gave a loud wail.

"I won't leave Vasily! Whatever he's done, Mama, I won't leave him."

Everyone looked around in considerable confusion, wondering who '*Mama*' might be.

Few noticed Lady Butterclere stagger for a moment as if about to fall.

She knew her game was now finally up!

Lord Radford whispered a few words to Henrietta and she nodded, a look of relief on her features.

"Lady Butterclere," he said, "it might interest Miss Foss that my daughter will not be pressing charges against Prince Vasily."

The Duke glanced at Lord Radford.

"That rogue had better leave England at once and for good!" he growled.

"He must marry Miss Foss first," put in Henrietta.

She was cognisant of the fact that poor Romany's reputation would otherwise remain in tatters.

Romany threw her a surprised and grateful look.

Prince Vasily nodded sullenly.

He and Romany rose and, without a further word, followed a cowed Lady Butterclere from the ballroom.

"I think I now understand – everything," muttered the Duke, gazing after them sorrowfully.

Henrietta bit her lip miserably.

She had no doubt that the Duke was also referring to her own deception.

Lady Bridgely gestured for the orchestra to resume playing. Onlookers began to drift back to the dance.

The Duke glanced at Henrietta and then took Lord Radford's elbow and led him to one side.

Henrietta felt Kitty take her hand.

"Harrie – I'll never stop calling you Harrie, – shall we go and take some refreshment?"

Henrietta shook her head and disengaged her hand.

"N-no, I just need to be alone for a while. It has all been t-too much."

Sobs rose in her throat as she turned away and did not hear Kitty's concerned reply as she launched herself in to the dancing crowd.

The Duke knew everything now! She never wanted to have to look him in the eye again.

She did not have the strength to decide her course across the ballroom floor as she was buffeted to and fro.

It was by sheer chance that she found herself before a set of French doors that led out onto a terrace.

Blindly she pushed through the doors, ran down the terrace steps and found herself in an ornamental garden.

Only now able to give vent to her feelings, she sank weeping onto a stone bench.

*

"You seem to have an odd predilection for weeping on stone benches."

Startled, Henrietta raised her tear-stained face.

The Duke, one hand thrust beneath his waistcoat, stood observing her with what seemed a cool detached eye.

Stung by his comment to the point of forgetting that she hoped never to have to meet his eye again, she sat up.

"And you s-seem to have a predilection for finding me out," she stammered. "When I do not w-want to be!"

The Duke's lips twitched.

"You seem to forget that the last time you resorted to this despair *en plein air* you became ill. Lucky I found you when I did."

'*Despair in the open air*!' she thought crossly.

"If you have come to m-mock me – " she began.

The Duke's gaze softened.

"I do hope you do not believe that, Miss Radford."

"You are mocking me again," she cried. "You have never known me by that n-name!"

"You seem to forget that I have. Long before I ever met Miss Reed, I was enchanted by Miss Radford. Though I have to say, she was a good deal more gracious as a seven year old than she is now!"

Tired, confused, her nerves stretched to breaking point by the dramatic events of the last few hours Henrietta now burst into tears.

"Why d-don't you just say it?" she wept. "You are – disappointed in her. She grew up to be s-someone who – pretended to be someone else – Miss Reed, who played the piano in an orchestra and d-dressed like – a saloon keeper's d-daughter!

"But you don't know – she only did that to h-help out E-Eddie and then it all got – *so* complicated – "

The Duke listened in silence.

He took out a handkerchief and knelt before the still weeping Henrietta and dabbed at her cheeks.

"Hush now, hush," he murmured. "I don't want you ill again."

Henrietta's sobs subsided but her breast still heaved with emotion.

The Duke's touch as he wiped away her tears was indescribably tender.

She stared at his face so close to hers.

"Y-your knees will get w-wet," she sniffed.

The Duke glanced down and gave a smile.

"Since I now find myself in this most convenient position," he said, "I should perhaps use the occasion to say what it is I came out here to say."

Her sobs were now mere hiccups of emotion.

"I h-hope it is not something – d-disagreeable."

The Duke repressed a smile.

"I sincerely hope you do not find it so."

He waited for a moment, his eyes becoming graver, and then he gave a sigh.

"Can you not guess, Miss Reed? I wish you to be *my wife*. Harrietta – Henrietta – will you marry me? I am so desperately and passionately in love with you."

Henrietta pushed him away and sprang to her feet.

"Henrietta – Harrietta! You see, you *are* mocking me."

She turned to run, but he caught her and swung her to him. She struggled against his breast.

"Do not flee away from me again, my darling!" he groaned against her hair. "You cannot imagine the agony I endured the last time you disappeared.

"You so intrigued me, so haunted my every waking moment. I came here tonight hoping against hope that you would be here with the orchestra and that I would find you – free."

"But you are not free yourself!" cried out Henrietta accusingly. "You are engaged to Romany. Why, even the night I was lost in the maze, it was after I discovered the two of you together."

"Engaged to Miss Foss?" he echoed in amazement. "Never, never, never, my darling, whatever my stepsister may have hoped. Why, that night in the garden, I had only taken her out there because she said she needed some air. And anyway she now seems to be much more taken by that ghastly Romanian Prince!"

Henrietta blinked.

"I don't know what to believe!" she wailed.

"My dear darling, believe this," rejoined the Duke softly, and taking her hand, he placed it over his heart.

She almost swooned as she felt his heart beating hard beneath his shirt.

"I did not know what to believe myself," continued the Duke. "I knew you were no longer with Eddie Bragg and I knew that as Prince Vasily became a confidant of my stepsister that you had rejected him too.

"I did not know the truth of your relationships to these two men until your friend Kitty told me this evening.

"The knowledge that you were innocent of all these charges against you both shamed and thrilled me," went on the Duke.

"Shamed me that I had ever doubted you. Thrilled me that it would be I and I alone who introduced you to the pleasures of love."

"B-but how could you m-marry someone who had played in p-public with an orchestra?"

The Duke bent his head to hers.

"Sweet creature, do you really think I would care about that? Times have changed a lot in England since you went away, don't you know! Besides, I do have my own form of punishment for such transgressions."

"W-what is that?" asked Henrietta fearfully.

"This," whispered the Duke as his lips met hers.

The feeling that burst through her veins was painful in its intensity.

She found herself longing to press closer and closer to the Duke's body, closer and closer until they melted the one into the other.

She utterly relinquished her struggle, allowing the Duke's strong grasp to lift her first onto tiptoe and then off the ground altogether.

At last their heads drew apart.

Panting for breath, their eyes locked.

"Let us be married as quickly as possible," groaned the Duke. "I must possess more than your mouth or go mad with desire."

Henrietta touched his lips with her finger teasingly.

"B-but who is it you wish to possess, Your Grace? Miss Harrietta Reed or Miss Henrietta Radford?"

The Duke roared with delight.

"Ah, my darling, you might be either and it would not matter. Both ladies have played upon me so artfully that I have been captured – body and soul."

He bent his head again to hers, pressing his lips to every inch of her face.

"Now, my angel," he murmured between kisses, "it is for me to play upon you!"

Henrietta thrilled at his words.

"I love you, Joe, I love you. You have captivated my heart and soul for now and for always."

Already she was responding with every fibre of her impassioned being to the mysterious and irresistible keys of love!